The Life and
Loves of Jet Tea

Joe Gardner

Cover photograph by Glen Strachan

Well Done
For being Welsh!

For the real Jet Tea and Maurice.

You know who you are.

Contents:

Tara

Jet Tea awoke with an erection. He lay cemented to a spot half-under his duvet; the room had just come into being around him but he wouldn't yet be able to interact with it as he couldn't yet move. His consciousness was only half-formed and remained that way for a short while as he slowly attempted to muster enough energy to shed his waking paralysis.

Eventually he groaned, forced himself onto his side and caught sight of the duvet-shrouded mound between his thighs as it slipped away, like a magician's assistant in a disappearing act. It seemed like the erection wouldn't subside any time soon, but he didn't want to take matters into his own hands, as Tara would be coming over in a couple of hours (which, incidentally was probably the motive for the erection in the first place) and he'd hate to tarnish the afternoon for both of them. It wasn't really a problem, either. He was solitary in his tiny little kingdom and there was no issue with presenting his sleep-given state of arousal to himself alone. Nevertheless, he'd have to get up eventually to cook his breakfast and see what the world had been up to while he slept. It was Thursday, so he doubted his mum was even in the house, as she usually worked Thursdays, but his sister may have been.

He rolled over onto his belly, arms splayed out over the pillows, in an attempt to flatten it. It was a short-term success as it bent down pressed between his leg and the admirably resistant mattress, but as soon as he moved again it would spring back up, proudly and defiantly.

As the final shreds of his waking catatonia wore away and getting out of bed became an achievable reality, Jet Tea beheld his dressing gown. If the appendage hadn't begun to find flaccidity by the time he wished to venture downstairs, he'd simply prop it up against his belly, then tie it in place with the belt of his robe. Simple. Nobody would suspect a thing, hopefully. He *could* make a quick trip to the bathroom for a direct extradition of the inconvenience; Tara wouldn't be here for a while yet and surely things would have returned to full working order by then? No. He'd feel more uncomfortable interacting with his relatives having recently done that than he would simply concealing a loaded weapon. It wasn't his fault that it was there, after all.

He got up, pushed the offending phallus up against himself, bent forward slightly from the mild pain of it and tied his dressing gown around it and his waist. Looking down, he could only make out the tiniest of protrusions amidst the shaggy fabric, and it was a lot higher up now so was much less likely to arouse immediate suspicion in the unlikely event that it was noticed by anyone.

Jet Tea left his bedroom with trepidation and went downstairs into the kitchen. Nobody was home, but either way the anxiety of his trip and the possibility of a family member spotting his guilty secret had paradoxically caused it to return to limpness – an inevitability he should have considered. He momentarily loosened his dressing gown to let things fall into their proper place then began to make his breakfast. It was, in actuality, close to one o'clock in the afternoon, so his meal was not strictly 'breakfast' in the eyes of conventional society, but given that he had only recently awoken, the time-frame of the day was still relevant to Jet Tea so it was breakfast to him, nonetheless. People on the other side of the planet were still yet to partake of their breakfasts, so his point was valid. Two Cumberland sausages glistened beautifully under their coats of sizzling-hot oil while a neighbouring saucepan full of creamy-white liquid bubbled away and eventually mutated into scrambled eggs.

Jet Tea took his breakfast upstairs, back to his bedroom, and put the television on. He flicked through channels past footage of blue skies and rolling green hills to a light-hearted, daytime documentary; *Mythbusters*. Before eating he changed out of his dressing gown and into a baggy t-shirt. Doing so, he caught sight of himself in the mirror. He looked proudly at his trim, youthful body, his chiseled and pronounced jaw line and his effortless, shaggy head of hair. His glasses enhanced his appearance and made him look intelligent in a handsome way; he glimpsed the copy of George Orwell's *1984* on the shelf behind him and smiled. Its presence complimented his aura of intellect. No wonder he was in love with a beautiful, mature woman who loved him equally in return. Jet Tea was deliberately self-deprecating most of the time; he considered it part of his charm, but today he felt amazing. A real man.

The phone rang. He answered it. His world ended.

Jet Tea met Tara one and a quarter years prior to the Thursday of the erection, the midday breakfast, *Mythbusters* and the phone call (exactly one and a quarter years, as he would later come to realise). They worked together at Fozzy's Lebanese Pizzeria and Other Foods in Pinner. He was an apprentice chef, having recently completed a food science course at Watford College, and Tara was a waitress on the brink of becoming assistant team leader. She was also fifteen years older than Jet Tea, making her thirty-seven when she began to grow fond of the timid, introverted, twenty-two year old chef.

Sex and romance had, up until this point, been of little concern or interest to Jet Tea, who filled the early part of his teenage life with neighbourhood and school friends throwing dairy products at buses and playing knock-down-ginger, and the latter part of it with college and work, both of which he enjoyed enough not to bother looking for a girlfriend. However, a previously unexplored curiosity awoke from a long slumber when he met a beautiful older woman who took a shine to him.

For Tara, who was already of a reasonable age to begin considering having children, the relationship with young Jet Tea began life as a kind of fond motherhood, but turned to physical attractiveness the more she grew to know him. It was also a matter of curiosity for her, who'd had as little intimate experience with younger men as Jet Tea had had with older women. As one would imagine, the difference in age was the source of immediate fun for Jet Tea's friends, despite Jet Tea himself not considering it unusual or unnatural in the slightest. It was not the source of fun for Tara's friends, as her then current simultaneous involvement in a long-term relationship with a media sales executive from Kenton called James meant she could not be particularly open or vocal about her budding love affair with Jet Tea.

This slight complexity meant that, despite their homes being an approximate six-minute drive from each other, Tara and Jet Tea would be compelled to take long, thrice-weekly tube journeys to Kings Cross to be with one another. Tara would only visit Jet Tea at his home if James's job forced him out of town for a few days. On those rare occasions, one would be lucky to see the door to Jet Tea's bedroom open at all.

On those precious few evenings during which

they would be able to spend time at home together, Jet Tea would delight in cooking Tara and himself a hearty, romantic meal. Although such a gesture is common throughout the worldwide relationship community, there was far more to cooking dinner for his girlfriend than being irresistibly romantic and ultimately enticing her upstairs; the prime thrill was in the cooking itself for Jet Tea, rather than the subsequent payoff. Having been enthusiastic about all things food preparation since a curiously early age, the culinary side of life had become Jet Tea's number one passion. That first sizzle of chopped vegetables hitting a greased frying pan, the grind of sea salt into the steamy, bubbling abyss of boiling pasta, the way a chicken breast shed its image of a dismembered animal part as it turned white on the grill; cooking, more than anything in his life other than Tara, literally made Jet Tea happy. During his time with Tara, Jet Tea would leave Fozzy's Lebanese Pizzeria and Other Foods, acquire a position in a three Michelin-Star restaurant in Swiss Cottage, have an unsuccessful job interview with Antony Worrall-Thompson and temp in the cafeteria of the school he used to attend.

Jet Tea's best friends were both musicians, and where he lacked a kinship with their kind of creativity, he excelled beyond them in the kitchen and that was his talent and his alone. Being creative with food would never fail to push Jet Tea's troubles to a dark, cloudy place seldom visited at the back of his consciousness. With this in mind, over a year later, one may perfectly understand why Jet Tea would solemnly regret cooking his breakfast *before* receiving a particularly upsetting phone call, rather than after. At least it would have numbed his despair somewhat.

Because of their constantly deviant liaisons, Jet Tea had to take out a rather large bank loan to pay for such things as bed and breakfast, romantic bistro dinners (during which he would never relent from begrudgingly commenting on the quality of the meat, the speed of service and how particular vegetables should have been cooked, silently envying Tara for her ability to just enjoy the meal) and birthday, anniversary and unnecessary greeting-card shop cash-in day presents. He was not overly bothered about the loan, because, quite simply, he was in love.

Five months after Tara and Jet Tea first made love, Tara opted to end her now virtually redundant relationship with the understandably distraught James. This decision drastically altered the nature and course of her formally simultaneous relationship with Jet Tea, for the two of them no longer had to travel across an absurd portion of the capital to be with one another, and it also meant that they could adopt a mutual social life, integrating with each other's circle of friends and not having to worry about being seen together outside of the house, or the Metropolitan line.

The first thing Tara's friends chose to notice about her new love was his age. This caused something of a friction in that Jet Tea's mentality was simply not yet in tune with their idea of a pleasant social event; which more-often-than-not consisted of drinking red wine and eating pitted olives at a cocktail bar in Ealing, whilst usually discussing mortgage payments and complaining that Craig still hasn't proposed, or implied that he will propose (for Jet Tea had decided that Tara's female friends' collective boyfriend was probably called Craig, and her two male friends that never really bothered involving him in their manly discussions were probably both called Craig as well. He wasn't sure why, he probably heard the name crop up in conversation during a particularly dull and arduous evening).

The second thing Tara's friends chose to notice about her new love was that he was quite clearly not enjoying himself on such evenings, nor was he attempting to engage with them on any level. Tara's friends were not attempting to engage with him on any level either, of course, but they steadfastly felt that it was not their responsibility to. Tara also noticed the first two things her friends noticed, but she did not allow them to burden her, instead she stored them somewhere within her psyche to be later conveniently revealed to her boyfriend on a day which saw her feeling lower and more irritable than usual. She did not, however, notice the third thing that her friends noticed.

The third thing Tara's friends noticed about her new love was that they did not like him. Furthermore, they liked Tara a lot less when Jet Tea was around, simply because it was solely her fault that Jet Tea was there, burdening their evenings with his ugly social and generational differences. When eventually Phillipa mentioned the third thing to Tara, amidst lamentations on Craig's new haircut, the possibility of such a relationship turning problematic first became clear.

The first thing Jet Tea's friends noticed about his new love was her age. However, being rather young, they did not react in the same way that Tara's friends did. It will come as a surprise to few that many a teenage boy and young man often wish to have some kind of an intimate experience with a woman who is older and more mature than he, and as such the mentality of Jet Tea's male friends in the company of Tara swung between curious awe and polite envy toward their fortunate friend. This was of course nourishment for Jet Tea's often starved ego, and the otherwise modest young man was pleased to discover that his relationship with an older woman was the most relentlessly talked about topic among his friends, regardless of Tara's actual presence.

On future nights out, Jet Tea would struggle to cope with not being a constant talking point, not because he was particularly egotistical, but because being talked about had become the norm, and it saved him the unpleasant effort of having to do something different for them to talk about, or ask them about how their music was going, which would cause the conversation to wander off into territory Jet Tea could not comprehend or contribute to, rendering him the proverbial 'third wheel.' Maurice and Hayden may not have been particularly talented chefs, but they could each comfortably hold their own in any conversation about food. Jet Tea would concur that whether or not a person actually knew anything about food, at least they liked to think they did. The same can be said for music, but Jet Tea had far too much integrity to pretend he knew more than he actually did about something, so would quickly tune out of any such discussion in a manner similar to how he would tune out of a conversation about Craig or mortgages with Tara's friends.

In meagre attempts to fill the eventual hole left by no longer talking about Tara, Jet Tea would either gratuitously bring her up in any conversation, regardless of her proximity to the subject matter, or do something outlandish and at random, such as choosing to be the only one in the pub to dance to the music (regardless of the actual presence of a dance floor, and which he deliberately did in the style of someone of the opposite sex in order to ensnare as much surrounding attention as could be), or raising his skinny arms high into the air and shouting at the top of his voice a falsetto incoherence, before collapsing in a fit of giggles as his sense of self-awareness gradually returned. If all else failed, he would do both of these things. This often worked too well, as it garnered not only the attention of his two friends, but that of everybody in the room, mistakenly leading to the general notion that Jet Tea was someone with extreme confidence.

The second thing Jet Tea's friends noticed about his new love was just how often she felt the need to argue with him. This would only occur when Tara would spend time with Jet Tea's friends, due to the heightened frustration she felt at being the oldest and therefore most mature person in the room, a frustration which often led her to persist in starting arguments for no reason. While Jet Tea would tackle his anxieties around Tara's friends by closing off and letting them get on with their evening by themselves, Tara was slightly less introverted than it is required to be for that kind of approach to work successfully. Instead, she would pick on any slight thing Jet Tea said or did, and express her disapproval, disdain, or disagreement with it. Jet Tea would then opt to defend his words or actions with more words or actions, resulting in a serious argument over a less-than-serious matter. For although Jet Tea was rather reserved in many confrontational situations, he was happy and comfortable enough with Tara to let her know the problems he had with her.

Maurice and Hayden perceived that this was the constant state of Jet Tea and Tara's relationship, as they had never observed the two of them in other environments (Jet Tea's friends and Tara's mixed only once, and on that occasion their relationship was considerably overshadowed by Maurice's drunken attempt to put his tongue in Tara's friend Gina's mouth, much to the annoyance of Craig). On drunker and more honest late nights, they would sometimes ask Jet Tea why he was even with Tara, to which he would angrily retort that they were wrong about her, and that they didn't know what she was really like which, of course, was true. But it is a fact of life that a drunk person knows more than anyone about anything, ever. Therefore the drunk Maurice and Hayden would shoot down Jet Tea's contention regarding Tara with angry self-assurance.

The third thing Jet Tea's friends noticed about his new love was that they didn't like her. Or rather, they didn't mind her, but they certainly didn't like the state that she put Jet Tea in when she was around. After the novelty of a candid view to an age-gap relationship and the wonder of what doing things to a naked older woman would be like wore off, Maurice and Hayden conceded that their friend was not happy, or particularly fun to be around, when Tara was present. When eventually Maurice mentioned the third thing to Jet Tea, the problems of a social relationship first became clear.

Eventually, Jet Tea and Tara stopped socialising as a couple, instead spending their time together in the privacy of Jet Tea's bedroom. Neither of them were particularly interested in watching films, and being constantly in each other's company meant they had little to say that the other would not already know, rendering conversation pointless (a problem), so they found themselves spending almost all of their time together making love. Jet Tea possessed the sexual eagerness of a young man, whilst Tara retained the sexual willingness of a middle-aged woman. These traits combined assured that the pair of them were rarely out of bed, let alone out of doors. The constancy of their physical intimacy led to Jet Tea routinely awaking in a state of arousal, purely in anticipation of a visit from Tara. This was basically an instance of Pavlovian sense memory.

This relationship was ideal for Jet Tea, who was simply having constant sex with an older, more experienced woman. He felt he was a teenage daydream made real, and that there was little need to change or rethink anything about his life with Tara.

Tara grew to think otherwise. While it may very well be the desire of many women close to forty to spend all their time on their backs with a young boy bouncing around on top of them, it was the desire of many other women close to forty to raise a family, with a financially dependable man of a similar age and therefore mentality to them, get married and live out the remainder of their days meeting friends for dinner, tending to their gardens and picking up their children from school. Unfortunately, Tara belonged to the latter group, and it was for that reason that one Thursday afternoon, at 12.46pm, three hours and twenty-four minutes earlier than she intended on arriving at Jet Tea's house for yet another day of rolling around naked with someone fifteen years her junior, she opted instead to call Jet Tea on his mobile phone.

But none of that mattered now, Tara was gone.

Jet Tea had felt no apprehension or alarm upon answering the phone call. His assumption was that she was probably phoning to ensure Jet Tea had an ample supply of contraceptives, or if he would like her to buy any food for dinner later. He did not at all suspect that she was calling to inform him that she would not be coming round any more, and that he would no longer be able to have sex with her, see her regularly or consider her his girlfriend. Due to the immense shock they were causing him, Tara's exact words were paradoxically inaudible to Jet Tea, but the essence of what she was saying was clear as day.

'Hello?' he answered, with the same combined tone of formality and familiarity that anyone adopts when answering the phone to someone whose identity is already known to them. Tara spoke, Jet Tea replied. 'What? … Why? … But, I love you … come round, come round and talk to me here … that's not true! …

Please come round ... Tara? ... Don't ... I love you.'
He fell back into the armchair beside his bed, as though
he had just been thumped in the gut. He had been, to a
degree.

Immediately, Jet Tea felt he should finish his
breakfast; perhaps as a means of comfort, or perhaps in a
meagre attempt to proceed with a normal, routine life.
Like an abused dog trying to continue eating from its
bowl whilst being repeatedly kicked in the ribs. After he
forced the last forkful of scrambled egg into his mouth,
he took his plate downstairs and then returned to his
bedroom, switched off his television, sat back in his
armchair and cried.

Shortly after he began crying, Jet Tea felt a hot,
sharp pain, akin to heartburn, poke at his chest. It didn't
so much clear, as subside slightly and take a perceived
back seat to the emotional pain he was feeling.

Jet Tea wept for what would have been the
remainder of *Mythbusters*, had he still been watching it,
then wiped his face with his dressing gown sleeve and
considered what his life would be from then on. He
stood up and looked in the mirror again. He beheld his
pathetically skinny body, his large head balancing on a
twig-thin neck; his overgrown mop-head and glasses that
made him look not unlike a boy wizard. He hadn't even

read the copy of *1984* that sat in his reflected periphery, and that made him feel like an idiot. Worse, an idiot so insecure with their idiocy that they must overcompensate and parade a fictitious intellect to people that really couldn't care less. No wonder Tara wanted nothing more to do with him. He was just a boy. A pathetic, little, crying boy.

The rest of Jet Tea's day was spent veering between soft crying and attempted sleep. Roughly an hour after Tara should have arrived (they'd just about be ready to go again, thought Jet Tea), his phone rang for a second time that day. It was Hayden, asking if Jet Tea would be at the pub later that evening. He replied before even wondering if he wanted to;

'Yes, I need to get pissed!' he told a pleased Hayden, before being informed that they would most likely get there for about 7 o'clock, a good hour to get seats but not be the only ones starting their evening.

He opted to walk to the pub, hoping his head would be clearer and more refreshed by the time he got there so he could drink more mind-numbing alcohol. On his way he thought about Tara, particularly her motives.

His feelings flowed from the initial upset he had felt all day, to anger at her cowardice in not meeting him in person, or allowing them to discuss the problem properly, for that matter. Then he briefly felt empathy for her, understanding her reasons somewhat, which somehow mutated to hope that perhaps it was just a temporary solution to an unrelated personal issue. That switched to self-deprecation at such optimistic naivety, which in turn became another kind of optimism, that now he had freedom and the possibility to meet somebody new and different to Tara. Then came the resignation that he didn't actually want somebody new and different to Tara, which was also upset once again.

He reached the big, looming doors of the pub. Laughter, incoherent chatter, soft music and the clang of glasses sounded from within. There were people in there, lots of people. People who, with two exceptions, didn't give a shred of a shit about what he was going through and thus wouldn't make kind concessions to him. They might laugh at his hair and glasses. The bartender might ask him for identification because even though he was in his twenties, he still looked like a fucking weedy little boy. Embarrassment, hostility and scrutiny were in plentiful supply beyond those doors.

But there was also beer, lots and lots of beer. And his two best friends in the world. These were both things he couldn't fathom going without right now, and no amount of hostility or scrutiny would outdo that need.

Without further hesitation, Jet Tea pushed the doors open.

Maurice and Hayden

'I keep telling people to commit suicide' said Hayden, absently sipping his pint. 'It's all to do with the law of averages, really. If I tell enough people, eventually one of them will.'

Maurice laughed. This was Hayden; forever mumbling pessimistic, on the nose remarks in a perpetual attempt to be more shocking than the people around him. They'd known each other for five or six years, and in that time Hayden's natural, introverted conduct had never really gone away, but had mutated into a sinister, quiet outlook on a world he was gradually growing tired of. He held a cynicism beyond his years; he never quite belonged to conventional society, but he could never completely escape it. He worked in a bar that largely catered toward hard-working admin and marketing types, so he found himself forever at the beck and call of smug, stylish suits that Hayden bitterly considered to be societal slaves, although they most likely considered themselves masters of their society. Either way, having unrolled twenty pound notes constantly waved at him by people spitting demands for whiskey and lager for forty six hours a week most definitely enriched his bitterness.

Hayden wasn't bullied at school like Jet Tea was; the 'cool' kids got on with him but generally left him to himself. Because of this adolescent mercy, Hayden was allowed time to think more. He considered himself a bit of a 'social ninja' (as he'd rather arrogantly put it), deliberately blending in with his dull clothes and short, dark hair. He'd even started wearing contact lenses instead of glasses, simply in an effort to abstain from any feature that might make him stand out for some reason.

'And what if everyone decides to take you up on your advice?' asked Maurice.

'If the entire world committed suicide?'

'Yes.'

'Then I'd probably sit down, enjoy the silence for half an hour then do the same.'

'How would you go about it?'

'I'd probably do something absurdly outlandish; there'd be no society left to hem me in for my behaviour, I'd have already won. The final act of human existence should most definitely be something completely extraneous to the recently deceased "conventional" society.'

'And what would that be?' asked Maurice, humouring his ridiculous friend.

'I'd strip naked and ride a motorcycle off of a cliff, singing *Let's Go Fly a Kite*' replied Hayden, with a swiftness that suggested he'd given it a lot of thought.

'Of course you will.'

Hayden's general outlook, particularly when under the influence of alcohol, was quite possibly in part down to knowing Maurice. For, although far more extroverted and comfortable in himself than either of his best friends, Maurice was also dubious of the society he lived in. In his circle he'd managed to form a sub-society, a collective consciousness, a herd mentality that was oil to the water of the general public's herd mentality. Whilst Maurice was content with this, Hayden had grown ever more bitter that they three were the exception to the rule. They didn't like the same music as most people their age, the thought of a two-week lad's holiday on a sunny Spanish island disinterested them completely, and they often found that their drunken antics were by and large at the behest of most people sharing the same space as them. Maurice enjoyed the fact that they lived largely off of the social grid, but Hayden always saw it as an indignation. Why should their way of being be the wrong way, when they were so much more honest with who they were? Why does the recognition of wrongful prejudice not extend beyond sexuality, gender and race?

There were reasons for Maurice's heightened comfort with who he was. He was the oldest of the three, by a couple of years. He possessed a bookish, bohemian charm that accentuated his already good looks and as such had the most success with the opposite sex. In most situations his savage honesty was lauded, rather than lambasted (Were he less pleasing to the eye, perhaps Maurice's confidence and honesty would be considered by most a horrid imperfection, for nobody likes being told what someone thinks unless that someone is 'a bit of alright.' There are those that see virtue beyond physical appearance, but they are, unfortunately, in the minority). He was also relentlessly intelligent, constantly able to make impressive contributions to any discussion and effortlessly bend that discussion into whatever shape he pleased. At times Jet Tea considered Maurice a member of that frustrating yet rare species; a know-it-all who actually knows it all. He also genuinely did not care what others thought of him. Jet Tea used to think the same of himself until he realised his concern that people weren't aware that he didn't care what they thought, which is of course a concern regarding external perception by default (Maurice had pointed that out to him on one drunken evening, and from then on Jet Tea was happy to continue pretending otherwise).

Hayden's passivity, on the other hand, affected his ability to talk comfortably to new people. Many mistook this for rudeness or disinterest and as such he was not as successful with the opposite sex as Maurice was, but there were those who believed he had a lot more success with the same sex. Nobody ever asked.

Maurice and Hayden had arrived at their local, the Treaty, a full eighteen minutes earlier than Jet Tea, who had told Hayden that he would be walking there. Eighteen minutes and the conversation had already descended into one about suicide, thought Maurice with a sigh. Jet Tea needed to hurry up and get here so as to offset the despair with his simple, happy-go-lucky brand of natural humour. As far as he knew, Tara wouldn't be joining them this evening. While Maurice liked Tara, he wasn't in the mood to play spectator to another trivial domestic.

Men that spend enough time together eventually develop a mutual beer-drinking speed not unlike the synchronization of menstrual cycles among women who have lived together for a while. Maurice and Hayden were each around half of the way through their pints by the time Jet Tea arrived. This meant that it was too early to accept Jet Tea's offer of a drink, for the latter would be warm and flat by the time the former had been finished. This was much to the emotionally distressed Jet Tea's relief, who was in no mood to carry three full pint glasses from the busy bar to their annoyingly distant table, shakily avoiding the wayward arms of giant, drunken louts who would inevitably turn their reckless spillage of Jet Tea's beers on their precious sleeves into his spiteful mistake, resulting in angry words and possible punches and head butts. Nor was he in any mood to ask someone for help, even if it was a simple favour of carrying one or two pint glasses to a table. Jet Tea did not want to come across as in need of anything, and once his friends learnt of what had happened to him that afternoon, his self-reliant exterior would be as convincing as John Keats telling a woman who had just learnt of her husband's affair with her sister that 'truth is beauty.'

They each spied their friend as he entered the pub through the main doors. Hayden was still engrossed in his rant about suicide and so he did not break his dialogue until he had finished his sentence, by which time Jet Tea had already sat down. Jet Tea, in turn, was slightly relieved that he'd managed to quietly slink to the table without being overly scrutinised by his friends. He didn't fancy much attention this evening. He rubbed his face; his eyes were slightly encrusted at the corners from where his tears had congealed with dust. He wiped the gunk away, wondering if his eyeballs were still tell-tale red from crying. Hayden finished ranting; Maurice wiped a rogue droplet of beer or saliva from his cheek that had been accidentally spat at him during the fervour.

'Alright, mate?' said Maurice.

Jet Tea nodded as nonchalantly as he could. ''Ello' he replied.

'How's Mum?' Said Hayden, for 'Mum' had, in previous weeks, become Maurice and Hayden's, and reluctantly, Jet Tea's inevitable nickname for Tara, due to her being older and possessing a tendency to give Jet Tea overwhelming care and attention. Of course, Jet Tea never used this nickname in front of Tara, except for on one unfortunately-timed occasion whilst being introduced to her own mum.

The topic had arisen far sooner than he'd hoped. He hadn't even sipped his pint yet. He bit his lip, leant back in his chair and stretched his arms, attempting to look as relaxed as possible.

'Yeah, yeah not bad' he mumbled.

Maurice and Hayden nodded, expecting that to be the end of the subject.

'Well, she dumped me today' Jet Tea continued.

Hayden's pint paused on its journey to his mouth as he gathered an expression of shock. He didn't know what to say. Maurice did.

'Why?'

'Yeah' said Jet Tea once again, rolling on the word with far too much indifference for the topic at hand. This adopted tone remained, to the discomfort of his friends, throughout. Furthermore, he hadn't answered Maurice's question.

'Mate,' Maurice seemed to ask, 'are you alright? I mean, you've been going out ages.'

Jet Tea was secretly hurt by Maurice's use of present tense, but of course said nothing of it. Instead he apparently shrugged off the last year and three months of his life with 'I wouldn't worry about it,' finishing off the moment with a slow swig of his pint for effect.

His friends were having none of his over-compensatory satisfaction. The ever-honest Maurice decided to tackle Jet Tea's tone with detached bluntness, perhaps the manner of an alien who has wandered into a group therapy session before being told that human beings can be quite sensitive about certain things.

'It obviously hasn't hit you yet' he said. Jet Tea fought off an astonished expression at this. 'How did it happen?'

'She rang me up this afternoon. Didn't explain much to be honest.'

'How did you take it?'

Jet Tea shrugged. 'I got over it'

'You got over it' said Hayden, splitting his sentence with a swig of beer but not breaking his curious gaze, 'in an afternoon?'

Jet Tea wanted nothing more than to kick down the flood gates and pile on all of his quivering, reined-in emotions onto them. He wanted to scream and fall helplessly onto Maurice's shoulder, asking why he deserved it and pleading through clenched teeth and floods of tears for both of them to make it better. But when they asked him how he was, he said 'not bad'.

Hayden shook his head in disbelief. 'Did she even give you a reason?'

'Said it was loads of reasons' Jet Tea replied. Maurice persevered with his blunt tone, which was perhaps less advised than before. 'Basically you're a cunt then.' His adjacent comical mode of delivery prevented this sentence from being a rusted kitchen knife into Jet Tea's already terminal heart.

Jet Tea had decided the conversation need go on no further. His friends knew that he and Tara had split up; they also knew that nobody other than Tara knew why, so there was no point pondering needlessly. A vet doesn't continually prod a headless toad in the hope of finding out how it has died. His attempt to change the subject was a temporary success. As the evening passed by they kept drinking, talked about drinking and how busy the place was getting for a Thursday, and attempted to tiptoe around Jet Tea's break-up until it became painfully clear that there was nothing nearly as interesting to talk about. Maurice was in the process of self-producing an album, and Hayden was trying, with little motivation, to write some new songs, but each of these things were completely trivial in comparison. Amidst this Jet Tea sipped casually on his pint in a useless attempt to look relaxed and at ease. He noted the looks of curious longing on each of his best friends' faces and decided that his stoicism was utterly pointless. It was time to open the flood gates once and for all.

'I just wish I knew her reasons' he revealed, lowering his head, his posture mutating into an honest one, and taking yet another swig of his pint, purely because he needed it this time.

Maurice placed a hand on his suffering friend's shoulder. 'You'll find out soon enough,' he said 'and then you'll realise she obviously wasn't worth the hassle anyway.'

At this moment in time Jet Tea felt like a fresh landmine victim being told his leg would grow back, but he had, in the past, seen Maurice in similar depths of despair and noted his eventual recoveries. As such, Maurice's words were of a slight reassurance to him. A smile found his face (an honest one this time) and Jet Tea would have felt a lot more relaxed if that hot stabbing pain in his chest would ease off.

A Wizard on Cowley Road

Cowley Road, which stretches from Uxbridge, West London, and through the unremarkable suburb town of Cowley, is a blank and purgatorial environment to walk through of an evening. Other than its countless rows of indistinguishable semi-detached houses, it harbours little more than a small Tesco's express, a pizza-delivery place and one or two off-licences. It would do well to have a violent reputation for muggings, stabbings and street gangs, but it can't even boast that. Cowley Road isn't even able to infiltrate conversation as a dangerous and scary place to find oneself, it is just dull.

Nevertheless, one Wednesday evening, Cowley Road somehow managed to become the setting for at least two life-changing events. For on that Wednesday evening a tall, beautiful woman with long auburn hair that waved gently in the wind took a walk down Cowley Road in order to decide whether or not she should make a phone call that would change the rest of her life. One may argue that she could have taken that walk down any road, but Cowley Road's lifeless, sterile atmosphere proved to be the perfect place for her to banish all environmental distractions and focus entirely inwards.

The woman had no intended destination, although technically her flat, from which she departed, was likely to be the journey's end. She just needed to take a walk and give her teeming brain a break from the surrounding cocktail of television noise, stuffy air and confinement that her home insisted on offering that evening. Outdoors was a much better place to be, which is something seldom said regarding Cowley Road.

It's amazing, she thought as she walked, how difficult it can sometimes be to do something you want to do with all your heart, if doing so would affect another person in any way. This extends further than selfish desire. It would be easier to accept this underlying feeling of preceding guilt if it only occurred when one intended to do something entirely self-serving and unnecessary at the cost of somebody else's well-being, but the troubling thing was that she was unquestionably certain that what she wanted to do would benefit everyone involved, which was actually just herself and one other person.

Despite Cowley Road's best efforts to be silent and uncharted, the woman's deep mulling was disrupted no less than twice. The first time, she happened to pass a particularly well-kept semi-detached house just as a similarly well-kept silver Ford Focus hatchback was pulling into its driveway. This event in itself would almost certainly have passed her by, were it not shortly followed by the emergence from the house of a lady of similar features and age to her, clutching a curious looking toddler. They had stepped out of the house in order to greet the man with short blonde hair and dressed in a long grey jacket, who was simultaneously emerging from the Ford Focus before planting an affectionate kiss on the lady's cheek, then another on the unflinching toddler's forehead. It was this moment that stole the woman away from her thoughts and caused her to stop dead in her tracks, staring intently at the scene being played out before her. Had they noticed the woman who stood motionless at the end of their driveway, the couple may have stared back, worriedly. They may even have asked her who she was or told her to go away. But, as it

41

happened, the two of them were far too happy to see each other to even notice her.

That brief moment happens a million times a day, all over the planet, and those it happens to have it happen to them almost every day. Yet, on rare occasions, the event is randomly witnessed by someone who has never had it happen to them and it strikes that person so deeply in the heart that it alters their entire future. That a minute expression of love between two people can have such an almighty impact on somebody that neither of them has ever even met is evidence enough for the existence of magic.

What makes this incident all the more fascinating is that the woman had indeed had it happen to her, countless times, to some degree. Except her experience of it exchanges the semi-detached house for a tube station, the hatchback for the northbound Metropolitan line service from Harrow-on-the-Hill, the toddler for a lukewarm big mac in a screwed up paper bag and, most crucially, the affectionate husband for a skinny, sexually-enthusiastic mop-haired lad in his early twenties. Measuring her version up against this far-and-away more idyllic scenario, the woman felt nothing but longing. She also found making that phone call would now be a great deal easier, were it not for the guilt. With this in mind she left the couple to enjoy the rest of their perfect lives and went on her way.

The second time her thinking was disrupted led to an interesting conversation that served to take care of the guilt concern. Deep in thought, staring anywhere but at the path ahead of her, she found herself colliding quite suddenly with a man travelling in the opposite direction.

'Ugh!' She gasped, upon impact.

'Watch it love', replied the man, angrily. It is interesting that whenever two people accidentally collide on the street, one always manages to entirely blame the other, despite the fact that it is only possible for the one placing the blame to bump into someone or something if they had not been looking where they were going either. It is also interesting, for the very same reason, that the person receiving blame will almost always say 'Sorry', which is precisely what the woman said.

The two of them were almost ready to part ways, when the woman took notice of the man's strange choice of clothing; a pink, long-sleeved, baggy T shirt almost completely buried under an absurdly oversized muddy-grey jacket. This untidy combination was made more bizarre by the inclusion of a pair of thin white gloves; and the thick, wiry gulf of dark brown hair that encompassed almost all of his head, leaving only his tiny, perfectly round eyes didn't help either. The woman presumed he was a few years younger than her, though it was difficult to tell with only a small portion of his face on display.

He had noticed her bemused stare; it was too late for her to hide that.

'What's wrong?' He asked.

'Sorry?' She replied

'Why are you staring at me like that?'

'Like what?' She said, slightly offended that someone with such an obviously attention-seeking appearance should feel the need to ask why people were staring at them. After a brief, uncomfortable silence she added 'What the hell are you dressed like?'

'Sorry?' He replied, not immediately registering how quickly the tables had turned.

'No' the woman abruptly intervened. 'Don't give me that.' In her defence she hadn't been caught at the best of times.

The absurdly dressed man said nothing.

'First you have a go at me for bumping into you,' she hissed, gesturing at the man and herself where appropriate, 'even though neither of us were looking where we were going, then you have a go at me for staring at you' she continued, 'despite the fact you

44

obviously dress like a twat to get some attention!'

Rather alarmed at what she'd just discovered herself of being capable of, she came to her senses and stopped herself from continuing. The man's overwhelming portion of facial hair made it hard for her to tell whether he was upset or afraid after her outburst.

'Sorry' she eventually said, and then, offering a friendly hand that was quite understandably left hanging in mid-air, 'nice to meet you, my name's Tara', to which the man said nothing and stepped aside to continue on his way. For one or two seconds they each carried on with their respective journeys until the woman stopped again, annoyed that all evening she had been placed at odds with what she felt she had the right to say, because of concern regarding other people's feelings. First, her as of yet unknowing boyfriend, now this moron.

Tara turned swiftly to the departing man and asked 'Why are you dressed like that?'

'I'm a wizard' he replied, without hesitation. Then he slapped his face in embarrassment and snorted 'I mean, magician.'

Tara said nothing.

A Little More About Jet Tea

'I bought this,' said Jet Tea, a tone of profundity and fondness in his voice and holding a paperback copy of George Orwell's *1984*, 'because it's the year I was born. It also looks good on the shelf, in case a girl is round.' Both of these statements were equally true, and Jet Tea has always maintained that, were he ever to overcome his severe dyslexia, he would actually read *1984*.

While his disability meant he generally didn't read books, Jet Tea was always attracted to literature. In fact his Myspace page, under the section titled 'About Me', read *'Dislyxci so dnt read, but if anyone got a bock to recomden let me no. Not 'Red Ridding Hod', read that'*. He even purchased a copy of Jerome K Jerome's

Three Men in a Boat and managed to read it. It took him four months, but he enjoyed it. Hayden once thought he heard Jet Tea reference Plato in an argument about American politics around the time of the 2009 Presidential election. What Hayden thought he'd heard Jet Tea say was 'Knowledge is the food of the soul; Plato', but they were drunk and in a loud pub and what Jet Tea had actually said was 'Porridge is on UK Gold later.' Nevertheless, Hayden has since maintained that Jet Tea would enjoy *The Republic*, particularly the bit about the cave, being a fan of *The Matrix*.

Like many, Jet Tea's dyslexia was mistaken, by lazy school teachers, for general idiocy and as such he was moved to the bottom class in every subject, a move that was based entirely on spelling rather than performance (he was doing very well in mathematics and science), and a colossal achievement in the eternal concept of institutional irony. Since suffering that indignity, and being witness to his outraged mother's fruitless tirades against the board of education, Jet Tea became somewhat jaded and disillusioned by authority and achievement. If nothing else, the British school system had inadvertently achieved the destruction of ambition in yet another young mind.

Despite this, Jet Tea retained his enthusiasm for

cooking, a field which, like the majority of the more creative pursuits, doesn't seem to discriminate against irrelevant learning difficulties. Ever since the day he was gouged from his physics class, Jet Tea knew that he would never be a stockbroker or a doctor, but cooking had always reassured him that, in certain careers it matters little what else you're good at, as long as you're good at the task at hand. Recalling an unsuccessful job application for an administrative office role, he could never quite figure out why a job that consisted primarily of transferring phone calls and filing mail required not only two years' worth of experience, but a university degree-level command of the English language.

Over the years, Jet Tea inevitably grew to accept his dyslexia. Among his closest friends he didn't even mind it being the subject of good-natured, mock-ridicule. In response to Maurice and Hayden discussing England's chances during the last World Cup, Jet Tea remarked, 'there's more chance of me reading *War and Peace*.' Whether or not that was the wittiest remark anyone had ever made was irrelevant, what matters is that it demonstrated how at peace Jet Tea was with his disability. He was a successful chef; not being able to read was about as damaging to his career as obesity is to a Science Fiction novelist.

His spelling was also a source of entertainment to his friends, particularly when misspelling words would accidentally cause his sentence to take on an entirely different meaning. For example, during a busy, twelve hour kitchen shift one day, Jet Tea managed to escape for five minutes to send Maurice this text message;

'*12 hors man. I feel like Im working in a Chinease Sweet Shop.*'

Other such messages included him asking his friends if they would be joining him in 'Condom town' on Friday and informing them that he 'bummed' into an old friend recently. Jet Tea was aware his spelling brought a childish smile to the faces of others but he wasn't particularly disgruntled by this. Any form of attention was, in his opinion, complimentary to his self-esteem.

Maybe in the future Jet Tea will figure out how to utilise his dyslexia as an adorable personality quirk that can add fuel to a conversation with a potential girlfriend. That was certainly the case with his name, which he one day hoped would catch the attention of a pretty Scottish girl named Gemma he'd soon meet in the pub.

Prior to meeting Jet Tea, Hayden's mum

naturally assumed he was an Asian martial artist. Whether this was result of a subconscious recollection of the actor Jet Li, or simply an assonant association with the East upon hearing the name is neither here nor there, but the fact of the matter is that Jet Tea is not Asian. His name, as has been established, isn't actually Jet Tea. But, in keeping with those frustrating few that seem to have their nicknames overtake their real names in terms of common usage, Jet Tea was almost never referred to by his birth-given name, except by his immediate family, his mother and sister, in the odd argument.

As it so happens, the name 'Jet Tea' was bestowed upon him by Maurice, moments after the two of them met for the first time on the tube. Jet Tea had, for an unknown reason, decided to formally introduce himself to Maurice using his first and middle names and his surname, and Maurice, being the instinctive drunken poet that he is, immediately fashioned the acronym 'JET', due to the fact that his three names begin with those three letters respectively. Contrary to subsequent assumptions, the nickname has nothing to do with aircraft, nor was Jet Tea remotely interested in aircraft. It eventually proved to be an annoyingly common refute by Jet Tea that, just because he worked for one week as a pastry chef at an airport cafe, his peers had named him

51

with aviation-based terms. The name was given several years before he began working at Heathrow.

The 'Tea' part of the name has less refined origins. The argument most commonly believed, and an insistence particularly maintained by Hayden, is that it is based on nothing more complex than Jet Tea's overwhelming love of tea. Even for someone born and raised in England, it is difficult not to pick up on the amount of times Jet Tea will offer you a cup of his latter namesake had you ever the pleasure of being his house guest. He quite probably drinks at least a full kettle's worth of tea each day, and that is excluding the cheap, unpleasant stuff he willingly and continually consumes during work.

A contradictory theory as to where the 'Tea' originates from has roots in the linguistic phenomenon known as 'RAS Syndrome'. RAS stands for 'Redundant Acronym Syndrome' and the inherent, deliberate joke within that term is that RAS Syndrome is itself a redundant acronym, in that the latter word used in the term is also the latter word that makes up the acronym itself. As such, if unravelled, it would read 'Redundant Acronym Syndrome Syndrome', in the way that ATM Machine would read 'Automated Teller Machine Machine', PIN Number 'Personal Identification Number

Number' and so forth. Where Jet Tea is concerned, the RAS Syndrome theory, held by Maurice (whose authority on the subject is arguably superior seeing as the name Jet Tea was coined by him), suggests that the 'Tea' is actually the first initial of Jet Tea's surname, used again to give the nickname a unique edge, and spelled the way it is to add something approaching symmetry to the name on paper (each word has three letters. It looks nice). As Hayden has little in the way of concrete proof for his argument, and Maurice was too inebriated to fully remember if his is correct, the matter remains unresolved. Although if one wished to offer support in the way of Maurice, it is important to know that he couldn't possibly have been aware of Jet Tea's fondness for tea having only met him for the first time, moments earlier. Perhaps new evidence will come to light one day in the more logic-and-reason-enriched future, but for now only one thing is particularly important, Jet Tea is Jet Tea.

Before he met Maurice, Jet Tea's nickname was Fish, because some think he looks like a fish. His eyes are sort of on either side of his head.

Jet Tea possesses a wit that is too quick for his mouth. As such he is capable of responding to somebody's shortcoming, as expressed by their fallible rhetoric, with deadly swiftness in his mind. However, such profound savage indignation seldom makes it to his lips intact, so Jet Tea often finds himself mixing his words, or using a well known catchphrase or tone of voice at a completely inappropriate moment. For example, a specific response to Maurice making fun of his dyslexia was the sarcasm infused 'yeah? Spell "get over it", jog on.' When he, Maurice and Hayden were discussing a mutual friend's constant refusal to show up at the pub or other such social events, Jet Tea's remark was; 'he doesn't even go to his own funeral.' It should be reiterated; Jet Tea has a firm grasp on the environment and is completely aware of people and his surroundings. His verbal responses occasionally suggest otherwise, but his wit is prominent enough for newcomers to instinctively perceive him as the 'funny one' of the group. His innumerable idiosyncrasies illustrate a strange, hyperactive and over-observant young mind that his words don't have to work to portray.

Gemma

The stabbing pain in Jet Tea's chest was growing stronger. While Maurice and Hayden were chatting in-depth about their appreciation of George Someone, the fifth Beatle (Jet Tea thought there were only four Beatles, and certainly only one called George), he was silently sipping from his pint glass, thinking about the day and becoming irritable. All of a sudden, a particularly noticeable strike stabbed Jet Tea in the chest, causing him to spit out his mouthful of beer all over the table, slam his glass down, tug violently at his shirt and stand up, almost involuntarily, supporting himself with one arm on the table and gasping in excruciating pain. A pain so immense it rudely has some sort of effect on other parts of the body, like when one bashes one's toe on the corner of a table or door and a sensation is felt halfway up the leg. In Jet Tea's case, the residual effect was on his ability to breath.

Maurice and Hayden's discussion was understandably terminated by this outburst, and they each stood up and sidestepped around the table to help their friend, though neither of them had the faintest idea what they should do.

Jet Tea had more than a faint idea of what they should do and, rather than telling them, he showed them. They should get out of his way immediately. With his help (a single arm displaying might beyond its unremarkable size), they did just that. The next few moments passed before most watching were able to register them, but for Jet Tea they seemed like the longest thing to have happened to him since a phone call he received earlier that day. He barged past Maurice and Hayden without a single word to them and headed for the gents' toilets, either unaware of or unconcerned by the series of people and pints he physically disrupted on his way.

To his frustration and lagging pain, the cubicle Jet Tea fully intended on entering as soon as possible was occupied. He learnt this when the door failed to respond to his shoving of it. Jet Tea had once heard that every action had an equal and opposite reaction, he would have liked to know where that reaction was when he needed it, because that door steadfastly refused to react to his pushing.

Then the pain became more severe because of the force he vainly applied to trying to open the cubicle door. Ah, he thought, there's that reaction. He silently apologised for questioning Newton's law of motion (though he wasn't aware it was Newton he was apologising to, of course) and proceeded to, quite uncharacteristically, bang against the door angrily.

'What!' came the response from within; it certainly didn't sound like a question.

Jet Tea did not reply, he was in too much agony to comprehend anything so complex as a sentence. He simply banged again.

'Fuck off.'

He banged again. Nobody else stood in the gents' toilets. Had someone else been present, Jet Tea may have behaved a little more inhibited toward his adversary in the cubicle.

'Fuck off' repeated the invisible enemy, before continuing; 'I'm having a poo.'

Several moments passed before the reassuring

thunderclap of a flushing toilet was heard from within. When it was, however, possible consequences of his abrasiveness toward the pooer hit home for Jet Tea. What if he was big? Jet Tea's skinny frame, Beatles-mop and reliance on glasses ensured he was seldom intimidating to even the more modestly proportioned gentleman. What if he wants to beat me up? If there was anything Jet Tea was in no need of stocking up on, it was pain. And beer.

Jet Tea would later congratulate himself for coming up with such an ingenious plan so quickly, and whilst in so much pain. He simply stood at the urinal, calmly placing himself in his own little world and miming the appropriate urinal usage. When the cubicle door finally burst open, and the as-it-so-happened large gentleman emerged, adorning a facial expression that could be described as disgruntled (but it wouldn't be doing it much justice), Jet Tea did not avert his gaze from the wall in front of him.

'Were you banging?' Asked the man

Jet Tea deliberately gave it a moment before feigning an ignorant response. 'Huh?'

'Who was banging on the door while I was in there?'

'Dunno mate' Jet Tea replied. 'I only just got in

here.'

The large man muttered an incoherent groan of resignation to himself and stormed out. Jet Tea made sure the door to the gents' was fully closed behind him before barging into the empty cubicle, locking its door immediately and slumping onto the toilet seat, which was kindly placed down (either that or the gentleman was actually using the cubicle to put things into his body, rather than get rid of them).

It is important to remember that Maurice and Hayden are faithful friends of Jet Tea's and, while he was in the gents' narrowly avoiding a thrashing from a recently-relieved large man, they were not simply carrying on their evening with disregard for their suffering friend. Being men first and foremost, neither of them opted to follow Jet Tea into the toilet. Whatever their intentions for doing that would have been, a group of men heading into the gents' together is never perceived well by onlookers. For women however, a group toilet-trip is the norm, sinister intentions or otherwise. The plan of action for Maurice and Hayden was to wait until Jet Tea returned from his trip and ask him, with full sincerity, if he was feeling okay.

Jet Tea eventually emerged. As Maurice and Hayden's mutual gaze remained steadfastly on the door of the gents' toilet, they were fortunate enough to witness the somewhat unbelievable following moments.

The door swung slowly open, and there he stood. His legs were placed slightly apart and his arm remained on the open door, keeping it that way. His body was cocked in a position resembling a frozen dance pose and his skinny face lowered, but not so much that it hid his intent stare and cheeky, sultry smile from them.

Jet Tea's friends stared in bewilderment at him as he remained in the doorway, an overpowering figure despite his bony frame, emitting a cheeky grin that let nobody know what had happened while he was in the toilet. His long fringe hung strategically over his glasses as he smiled insanely at his friends across the room.

Then things got stranger.

Silently deciding that he liked the music that was being played, Jet Tea let go of the door and made his way back to the table, through the means of some kind of incomprehensible dance. His focus remained on Maurice and Hayden and, as he boogied closer, his smile widened to reveal some teeth.

Hayden's face twisted into something between a smile and a concerned frown as Jet Tea took his seat.

'Feeling better?' he asked.

Jet Tea's reply wasn't worded, but it made his point clearly. He let out an enthusiastic, high-toned giggle and leaned into Hayden, poking him in the chest and stomach repeatedly, before leaning back, comfortably supporting his head with his hands. Maurice and Hayden laughed. Jet Tea finally spoke.

'Yeah I'm feeling pretty good as it goes' he said. 'What are we doing now?'

Maurice looked unsure. 'What do you mean?' he asked.

'I mean' Jet Tea continued, 'shall we go somewhere else, or-' he trailed off.

'I don't know' Maurice replied. 'It's alright here, isn't it?'

'I was thinking we could go into London' continued Jet Tea.

Hayden looked troubled. 'I'm not dressed for London' he said. Jet Tea's reply came in the form of an uncaring wave of his hand that strove to dismiss concern for anybody's dress sense. Contrary to the understanding of many, there are actually places to drink in central London where looking like you've just stepped off of a page of *GQ* magazine isn't a requirement.

Maurice had had enough. 'Mate' he said. It is

advisable to start a sentence with 'mate' if you are an English male, it adds sincerity. 'Are you alright?'

'Yeah' said Jet Tea elongating the word with far too much relaxation. 'Why?'

'Well you rushed into that loo looking like you were about to vomit' said Maurice, 'but now you seem happier than ever. What's up?'

'Ah don't worry about that' Jet Tea replied, 'don't worry about that.'

In actuality, what really happened in the toilet was something that should be worried about. Once Jet Tea had taken his seat and was certain that the angry man who said he was having a poo was not going to return, the first thing he did was slump forward. He extended an arm and leant it against the wall in front of him to stop himself from falling off of the toilet seat completely.

The next thing he did was take a deep breath, while staring at the damp floor beneath him. Then he screwed up his face and cried. It may not be essential to raise alarm at the crying of a man who had been dumped by his long-term girlfriend that very same day, but Jet Tea did not just sob and shed the appropriate amount of tears, he tugged at his face, quivered in his seat and screamed through gritted teeth, knuckles turning white as his fists became clenched as tightly as his pain threshold would allow.

Tara wasn't just on his mind, she was in his head. Jet Tea, growling tearfully, face-in-hands on a pub toilet seat, was utterly convinced that the physical form of his recently ex-girlfriend had literally managed to find a way into his brain, for she was standing as clearly in his mind as the opposite wall would have been to his eyes, were they open. The tiniest nuances of her face, every imperfect fibre of her clothing. He could even feel her breathe.

In his head, Tara smiled. While she smiled she opened out her arms. After she opened out her arms, Jet Tea seemed to also arrive in his head, critically being able to physically penetrate his own mind. For several seconds Jet Tea was unsure whether he was still on that toilet seat, or if he had indeed completely folded in on himself and henceforth only existed in what recently ceased to be his mind and was now an independent consciousness, a new substitute for an evermore unattainable reality and dreamed up by a now non-existent crying man.

Then the internal Jet Tea stumbled into the internal Tara's open arms, almost collapsing onto her

63

supporting body. Her arms slowly closed around him, tighter and tighter, and she planted a loving kiss on the top of his head, which was mostly buried in her chest. It was the softest and warmest kiss he could ever imagine, and he could feel her smiling sweetly through it.

Then the external Jet Tea, who, it has since been established, was still existent on the pub toilet seat, opened his eyes and looked up. He was certain he saw the fluorescent light slide back to where it should have been in the first place. Not the light being emitted, but the solid, plastic casing itself. He realised that all this time he had been constantly groaning. Jet Tea wiped his face with the front of his T shirt, and then found his face falling back into his hands.

This time he couldn't see Tara. Not only that, but he could not, no matter how hard he tried, picture her in the slightest. Not in the previous, disturbingly physical presence, nor in any partially formed, distorted mental image. His mind knew what she looked like, and could conceive and understand her in her correct shape, but for some reason, no shred of an image could enter Jet Tea's head. It was as though Tara had become unthinkable, unimaginable. Regardless of his utmost mental straining, he couldn't remotely picture his ex girlfriend.

Then he opened his eyes again and sat back, feeling disturbingly calm. Then he felt more than calm, comparatively, calm quickly became a negative feeling to what Jet Tea began to feel. He began to feel hope; overwhelming, unquenchable hope.

'I think we should stay here' said Maurice, observing his surroundings. 'It's beginning to pack out a bit anyway.' Hayden nodded in agreement. It was indeed getting busier. Despite his earlier expressed desires to head toward more exciting pastures, Jet Tea seemed extremely content in his acceptance to remain in the pub.

'Fair enough' he said, before offering to buy the next round of pints. Maurice's grateful eyes followed Jet Tea up from his seat and away from the table, and on their return journey they caught sight of a pretty young lady, sporting a mousy-blonde ponytail and a black and white striped scarf, whose eyes also seemed to be following Jet Tea to the bar.

The mousy-blonde haired young lady whose eyes had been following Jet Tea seemed to strategically manoeuvre herself into his return journey once he had purchased the pints. On his return, he finally caught a glimpse of her interested stare himself and returned it, albeit in a more confused and unprepared manner than hers. He decided that the successful delivery of his friends' pints was still his top priority, and returned to the table.

'There's a girl over there' said Jet Tea cautiously.

Hayden blinked. 'There are lots of girls, Jet Tea' he replied.

'No' Jet Tea persisted, 'there's a girl who smiled at me.' As a matter of fact, the girl wasn't smiling at him, simply staring. But Jet Tea's memory altered the fact for his own convenience.

Maurice leant into the conversation. 'I noticed that' he said.

'Maybe I should say hello?' said Jet Tea, turning thoughts into questions with the tone of his voice. 'Maybe she fancies me?'

'Or' Maurice began, 'maybe she just saw you dancing like a twat out of the toilet.' His intention wasn't so much to insult Jet Tea as to keep him from getting his hopes up.

'Nah' Jet Tea replied, almost giggling, 'she wants me.'

She Wants Me. Jet Tea had arrived at this conclusion on the back of three factors; noticing her

66

looking at him, incorrectly remembering her flashing a smile and being told by a third party that she was indeed looking at him. Jet Tea knew not who this mysterious lady was, he had not spoken to her, or even heard her speak at this point, but the optimism he'd picked up in the men's toilets had allowed him to convince himself into believing that someone he didn't know was in love with him.

From that moment on Jet Tea searched his mind for a conversation starter. He scampered about frantically, turning over various 'how's it goings' and 'let me buy you a drinks' and digging through the untidy pile of chat up lines he thought he had learnt from men's magazines but had possibly made his own alterations to via forgetfulness, such as 'do you believe in love at first sight, or should I just walk away?' and 'are you an angel? Because you fell off a Christmas tree', but he could find nothing satisfactory. Perhaps the perfect conversation starter was wedged down the back of the settee of his self-confidence.

Then he remembered he had an unusual nickname.

Maurice and Hayden watched in bewilderment as Jet Tea swallowed at least half of his pint in one go, stood up and walked overconfidently toward the girl, who by now had stopped staring at him and had returned her attention to the friends she was with.

'Hi, I'm Jet Tea', he said.

The girl's friends responded with a small variety of confused stares before she had actually turned round. She had noticed his approach in her periphery, but hadn't bothered to immediately act on it. Either thankfully or unfortunately, this did not deter Jet Tea.

She turned around to meet his big smile. 'Erm,' she muttered, 'hello, Jet Tea.'

Her accent told Jet Tea that she was probably Scottish. An image of the Loch Ness Monster swimming along happily immediately flashed in his mind, followed by Ben Nevis. But because Jet Tea didn't actually know what Ben Nevis was, only the words appeared in his mind, in big white capitals, with 'Nevis' spelled incorrectly.

'Not bad, thanks', replied Jet Tea to a question that was never asked. 'What's your name?'

'Gemma', said Gemma with a smile. More a polite smile than an affectionate one, but a real, unimagined smile nonetheless.

Jet Tea was quietly alarmed that Gemma had not yet asked him about his nickname, but persisted anyway. He held out a hand for a handshake and said 'nice to meet you Gemma.'

Gemma accepted the handshake. 'Nice to meet you too, Jet Tea' she said. 'How's your night going?'

'Not bad. My girlfriend dumped me today and I nearly got beaten up in the toilet' Jet Tea replied. The majority of people attempting to woo a lady would most likely have reserved these two facts until later in the conversation, when the initial small talk had subsided, but for some reason Jet Tea's newfound confidence was currently outweighing his self-awareness at a commendable rate.

Gemma raised her eyebrows and dropped her smile upon hearing this. 'Blimey' she said, 'are you okay?'

Jet Tea winced and waved a dismissive hand. 'Yeah' he sighed, 'nothing to worry about.' His gaze was placed steadfastly on Gemma and as a result he hadn't noticed her friends perplexed, disapproving glances.

She giggled nervously. Her end of the conversation was, though friendly in tone, strictly formal. She had told him her name, said it was nice to have met him and shaken his hand, but for some frustrating reason, this stranger with the odd nickname seemed convinced that they had become mutually

69

engaged in a deep and meaningful conversation, despite it only having begun barely over a minute ago.

'She didn't give me a proper reason' he lamented, realising that he was only feigning the self-pity and dwelling thought he was attempting to get across. He wasn't even actually thinking of Tara as he spoke. 'That's what's annoying more than anything.' Before Gemma could offer a response, Jet Tea continued. 'Are you Scottish?' he asked.

Gemma hesitated. 'Erm, yes. I'm from Paisley.'

'Are you on Holiday, or do you live here?'

'I live here, actually' she replied. 'I transferred from my old job.'

Jet Tea kept on with the questions. The conversation had changed into something resembling a job interview, which perhaps wasn't the best direction thus far but Jet Tea was undeterred.

'What do you do?' he asked. He actually despised talking about work. Although he loved being a chef, to him a job was something you do in order to get through life comfortably, not something that should define you as a person. He was always somewhat confused when Tara would, after a bad day at work, spend all evening complaining about her day. Surely the best thing about a working day is the fact that, at the end of it, you don't have to be there anymore? Why use up the good part of the day reliving the bad part? There are other things one could be doing.

'I'm a nurse' Gemma replied.

'Is it fun?' asked Jet Tea, 'my aunt's a nurse.' That was a lie.

'Yeah, I like it' said Gemma, unconsciously becoming a little more settled in the conversation. 'I work in paediatrics so I don't have to deal with much of the horrible stuff.'

'My job probably keeps you in business' Jet Tea said, preparing to attempt a joke. Several people had told him he was funny, so he occasionally acted on this reputation.

Gemma looked confused. 'Why, what do you do?'

'I give people food poisoning' Jet Tea replied, trying to suppress a laugh.

'Huh?'

'I'm a chef' he said, and thus the joke was complete. It didn't get the hearty, genuine laugh he was hoping for, but he'd completed a joke without fumbling his words or laughing at himself and the slightly forced giggle that Gemma offered as an act of courtesy was good enough. In the meantime, Gemma's friends had wandered off.

'A chef' Gemma echoed. 'That's cool, do you work anywhere nice?'

'Sometimes. I work in a school dining room right now.'

Gemma nodded slowly, wondering whether Jet Tea was simply a cook who felt the need to dress up his job title in order to impress people. This occurred to Jet Tea also, who acted quickly.

'I had an interview with Antony Worrall-Thompson once' he said.

'Oh' said Gemma, 'is he the little ginger one?'

'Yeah. I didn't get the job.'

There was an awkward pause as neither of them was sure where the conversation was going. Gemma disrupted it. 'I'm sorry, what did you say your name was?' she asked.

Jet Tea wondered why his unusual nickname had not made an impression on her. He was relying on it to ignite her interest. Nevertheless, he reminded her.

'Where'd you get a nickname like that?'

Time passed. Beer flowed. Perceptions shifted. Reactions heightened. Maurice was coiled on the dance floor, screaming at the DJ for some early Beatles songs, though the defiant DJ dismissively refused to play anything that would so much as make a sixth-former feel young. Over in the corner of the room, Hayden was slumped on the table with his head buried in his arms. He was either crying or passed out.

To Jet Tea, however, these things were as impacting as those portraits that aren't quite interesting enough to turn your head in an art gallery. His focus was entirely on Gemma all night long and to his delight, her focus was entirely on him. They had managed to navigate safely through the early stages of a first conversation and were now actually enjoying talking to each other, each telling interesting stories that the other was genuinely happy to listen to.

Anyone who has ever experienced a really good night out at a pub will know that the ring of the last bell and the increase in room-lighting at the end of the night is an experience not unlike being rudely awoken from a wonderful dream. It instantly drags you out of the pleasant reality you've created for yourself and dumps you back in the real one, the one that you have no control over and aren't allowed a say in how it unfolds. The reality that someone you don't like chose the wallpaper for. When this happened to Jet Tea he clenched his teeth and managed a polite smile. He didn't feel he had reached a satisfactory crescendo in the impression of himself that he was gradually building, but at least Gemma seemed pleased to meet him.

Maurice, while being ushered from the building by a bouncer that seemed to have come from nowhere, caught a glimpse of Jet Tea standing by the bar, opposite that girl he was speaking to earlier. In his intoxicated quest for a Beatles song he had forgotten about his friend's pursuit, but was amazed to see that after several hours the two were still communicating and appeared to be currently exchanging mobile phone numbers.

Hayden was brought back to reality not by the bell or the increase of light, but by a persistent tapping on his shoulder. His head shot up from the table to meet the concerned stare of a barman, or a sympathetic customer. He was too drunk and hazy to know or care. Despite this, he still managed to retain the memory of Jet Tea and the girl he was talking to, embraced in a goodbye hug. Hayden forgot most of the evening, but not that.

Jet Tea left the pub with a big grin that may as well have been tattooed on for all it was likely to ever move. Though he managed to escort a severely drunken Hayden to his house (for Hayden's house was too far away for him to successfully get there in the state he was in) and send a concerned though misspelled text message to Maurice, who he had not seen leave, Gemma remained on his mind constantly, until he fell asleep. He hadn't thought of Tara once since his episode on the toilet.

Tara and the Magician

Tara, alone on a dark street, had just met a strangely dressed man who told her he was a wizard, then swiftly corrected himself with the more socially plausible 'magician'. There were no other people in sight and the man, who looked athletic enough, was standing rather close to her. Furthermore, Tara had, not two minutes ago, all but called this man a total arsehole.

Thankfully, for the last one and a quarter years Tara had been in a relationship with Jet Tea, so was more than used to dealing with bizarrely-dressed young men who behaved strangely.

With admirable swiftness, Tara armed herself with two flippant replies to the man's claim that he was a magician. She used them both, in quick succession.

'Show us a trick, then' was the first.

'Do you know David Blaine?' was the second.

The supposed magician looked insulted and huffed.

'Yeah' he said, 'everyone thinks I'm a dick head.'

'I never said that,' replied Tara

'You called me a twat'

'It's not the same.'

The magician swayed in frustration, and tried to lean into a step to walk away, but found he had actually become a member of a conversation and, as such, doing so would be impolite.

'I've actually had a rather bad evening' he said.

'Why?' asked Tara. 'What happened?'

The magician evaded the question. 'I'm on a walk to clear my head.'

'Me too' said Tara.

'What for?' asked the magician, despite ignoring Tara when she asked him the same.

Tara took a deep breath. 'I'm thinking of breaking up with my boyfriend.' She realised that was the first time she had said it aloud. 'In fact I'm almost definitely going to.'

The two of them stood in silence, neither

entirely sure why they hadn't yet parted ways. The magician spoke again.

'Guess what I did.'

'What?'

'I did a bad trick and they kicked me out of my magic club' he said, almost with an undertone of mischief to his voice.

Tara politely restrained herself from emitting a sigh at that remark. Instead she decided to humour the man. 'What did you do?'

'Something against the law' he replied, darkly.

'What, illegal?' asked Tara.

'No, no' he said, 'the laws of the magic circle.'

Tara nodded slowly. 'Oh yeah, I know' she said, 'like when you give away how tricks are done to Joe public and they get annoyed.'

'Not quite' the man mumbled.

Tara, suddenly robbed of the short-lived sense of relief that she was talking to a mature and sane man who just happened to have a job as a party magician doing card tricks, finally let out that sigh. The magician lowered his head.

Without looking up at her, he spoke. 'Nobody believes me' he said. 'And they never let us prove it.'

Tara took a slight step back. Jet Tea had never

reached this level of oddity and she didn't know how to respond.

'But they don't want me any more and I can do what I like' the magician continued.

'I'm alright, really' said Tara, nervously. 'I've seen card tricks before.'

She suddenly realised that, from the moment the magician lowered his head, everything around her felt different. There was no change in the weather, and the sky didn't become any darker, but both of those things felt to Tara like they had in fact happened. She felt as though she was standing in a midnight storm, that the stranger before her was hovering several feet above the ground and shouting into the wind and rain, thunder drowning out his words but at the same time giving them significance.

'I have so much to show people' he cried, 'I'm superb at what I do and what's the point in keeping it a secret?'

But there wasn't so much as a light breeze down the Cowley road, nor had it rained in several hours. Nothing had visibly changed.

The magician raised his head, and the storm that never happened ceased to rage. For some reason, Tara no longer felt like she was talking to an idiot.

'So what was the trick?' she asked.

'What's your boyfriend's name?' came the inappropriate reply.

'Jet Tea.'

'That's an odd name.'

'It's just a nickname' said Tara. 'His real-'

The magician interrupted. 'You want to see the trick?' he asked, seemingly happier than in recent minutes.

Tara felt uneasy. 'Erm, didn't you say it was illegal?'

The man laughed dismissively. 'What I do has nothing to do with the law of the land' he said. 'Not for a few decades yet, anyway.' This comment did little to quench Tara's uneasiness. She stood silently for a second or two while she attempted to mentally construct the best reply to that sentence.

'You sound like you know the future' she said, sounding a little more sincere than she'd intended.

'I can still smell it' he replied.

Tara huffed. It was now beyond all doubt that she was talking to a lunatic, but at least a pretty harmless one.

'Smells linger in clothing,' said the man, 'loud noises leave a ringing in the ears.'

'What are you talking about?' asked Tara politely.

'Anything that has a large impact leaks out into whatever surrounds it' he replied, continuing his nonsensical monologue. 'But an event, a happening in time with a profound impact on history, well that has nowhere to leak into,'

'Okay, so was it like a coin trick or-?'

'Except backwards and forwards in time.'

Tara suddenly realised she was shaking her head softly. She stopped. 'Well I have to be off' she said, somehow less politely than when she asked the man what he was talking about.

'Hang on' shouted the magician. He held up a small square of card in his hand and offered it to Tara. 'The trick' he said.

Tara took it, she turned it around.

It was a photo of her and Jet Tea.

'That was in my purse!' cried Tara. 'You went through my stuff!'

The magician bit his lip, trying not to display guilt on his face. 'I took nothing else' he said, defiantly.

Tara snatched her purse from her pocket and scoured through it. She then glanced accusingly at the man.

'Nothing else is gone' she said suspiciously, stuffing the photo back into its correct place. 'That is a bloody good trick, though I can see why it got you in trouble, going through people's things and that.'

The magician giggled. 'That? That wasn't the trick' he said. 'That's *a* trick. Were you listening to me just now?'

'What? When you were babbling about history?'

'What I was going to say,' he replied irritably, 'is that at some point in a few years' time, something about the cosmos will change. Magic will become real, most of the illusionists and party magicians will be out of a job. The better ones will maintain the firmest grasp on this new force and become wizards.'

'…' said Tara.

'This event will have such a profound impact on the universe that it's leaking. Leaking backwards through time. I don't know what caused the magic, well - I might know, I haven't asked.'

'What does that mean?'

'It means there is a slither of magic that exists right now, and my group were among the first to utilise it. Little things about the atmosphere can be manipulated, tricks can be done. When I picked up that photo, I hadn't physically been into your purse. I made myself susceptible to the mental images of your boyfriend that were radiating from your consciousness and used them to allow the closest physical thing that bares his image to materialise in my hands.'

'You' Tara said, 'are talking complete bollocks. You pick pocketed me when I bumped into you, that's all.'

The magician smiled a smile that suggested she might have been on to something with that last remark. 'Your face when I was complaining a minute ago' he said.

'What about it?' asked Tara.

'You looked terrified. I wasn't saying anything particularly unnerving, and I'm not a particularly big man. Why did you look so scared?'

'I-' Tara attempted to reply.

'It's because my emotions were manipulating the space around me. That's how it works. You probably experienced a sense of increased darkness, or a change in the weather. It didn't actually happen, but your senses were bent in that direction.'

'It was a little odd' Tara admitted.

'Well in the future I'd probably be able to actually make those things happen. There may one day be real storms and real darkness when I get angry.'

Tara didn't particularly like the sound of this. She ignored the last comment.

'So what was this trick that was so bad it makes going through a woman's purse look acceptable by comparison?' she asked.

The magician sighed and smiled. 'You want me to show you?'

'Yeah' said Tara. 'Why the hell not?'

So the magician showed her, and he was right. It was bad.

Later on, Tara went home and climbed into bed. She had made up her mind; tomorrow she would phone Jet Tea.

That night there was a horrendous thunderstorm.

Jet Tea is Let Down

Guilt. Shame. Unrelenting despair periodically staved off by healthy doses of the alcohol that is paradoxically responsible for said guilt, shame and unrelenting despair. This, to his headachy, twitchy chagrin, was most definitely Hayden's modus operandi. He lay in his twisted pants on an unfamiliar, chilly bed among whiskey stains and strained memories, groaning internally; waiting for all the terrible, terrible things he'd most certainly done last night to return to him.

Then they did. With a sudden alarm that may or may not have caused his head to explode he swung for his phone. Facebook; the technological equivalent of that cunt of a sober friend that smugly reminds you what a drunken idiot you are and then announces that idiocy to everyone who wasn't there and would have otherwise comfortably escaped that revelation were it not for them.

The post read; 'All those thinking of donating to *Help For Murderers* why not just save money and kick a black kid to death instead?'

Jesus Christ.

No. Facebook isn't that teetotal wanker. Facebook is the physical embodiment of one's own internal thoughts. The mind, whored out to the digital world for all to see, with its diseased genitalia on display and everything. *I think, therefore I update.* You can think these things with a sober mind, but the only way to ensure drunken thoughts are maintained is to record them.

Hayden tried not to look at the forty-three comments dangling from his status, but he involuntarily glimpsed a few. There were plenty of capital letters and 'fucks' and 'cunts' from otherwise well-wishers. One read; 'YOU ARE SUCH A WANKER HAYDEN. DON'T YOU KNOW THAT THE BRAVE MEN AND WOMEN YOUR SLAGGING OFF DIED FOR YOUR FREEDOM OF SPEECH'. All of them? If that freedom of speech is so precious that it's worth dying for, why would someone get so terribly angry when it is put to use? He deleted the status and, momentarily at least, the deed was erased from existence.

But why all the anger? Hayden asked himself in an attempt to offset some of the personal shame. Why is someone else's relatively harmless personal opinion so often met with violent outrage? Hayden wasn't accusing anyone of kicking black kids to death, nor was he endorsing it or admitting to ever kicking black kids to death. Furthermore the recommendation, as it was framed, was so obviously sarcastic that there would be no way on Earth any of his friends would mistake it as genuine advice, would there? As far as he knew, Hayden was never mistakenly identified as a regular advisor on how to get rid of defenceless minority groups, so why would anybody make that mistake now, on facebook at two in the morning?

Perhaps the absurd fury met with any kind of comment that is remotely anti-military stems from the insecurity of people being forced to question why they believe what they believe. No matter how much conviction one has towards one's own moral stance, a radical counter-argument will cause one to question it. Nobody likes to learn that their entire, life-long moral code is society-structured bullshit. Or else comparing soldiers, 'heroes' in the eyes of most, to people that enjoy kicking black kids to death is not a very popular comparison.

Good old Jet Tea, infamous technophobe. He would be blissfully unaware of Hayden's brief foray into black-kid-death-kick advice. To Jet Tea, facebook was something some other people chose to do, like smoking or watching crap, emotionally-fractured singers get laughed at by millionaires on television. Of course, to people who partook of those things, they were essential in a way nobody who abstains could ever understand. It's all well and good for red-faced, right wing non-smokers venting their livid confusion as to why homeless people 'don't just give up smoking', but an addiction will really only ever be understood by an addict. Jet Tea genuinely didn't understand the point of facebook. On mornings like this, Hayden agreed with him. He chucked his phone on the floor and slammed his face into the pillow to begin his journey back out of reality. Then the door opened.

Jet Tea was awoken by a familiar voice in the next room. It was his mother, screaming in shock. As he regained complete consciousness, he suddenly remembered where he had left Hayden, who was so very intoxicated the night before. His door opened.

'Your sister's room?' asked his mother, angrily, before leaving without another word on the subject.

Jet Tea slithered out of bed and stumbled into the bedroom next door. There, tangled in his sister's previously well-made bed sheets and wearing only a thin pair of boxers that had become tangled around various body parts, lay his drunken friend. Jet Tea grabbed the closest thing to him, a soft alligator toy, and hurled it at Hayden, who, with some considerable difficulty, lifted his face from the pillow.

The two friends sat in Jet Tea's room, staring at a loud but unremarkable American sitcom on the TV.

'You need to start putting me on the sofa' groaned Hayden.

'You need to stop falling asleep on the bus so I don't feel so bad about letting you go home by yourself' replied Jet Tea.

Hayden nodded with reluctant agreement. He most likely held the record for most nights spent in a woman's bed without actually having ever met the woman in question. He wondered if Jet Tea's sister, who in turn spent most nights round her boyfriend's house nowadays, even knew that there was a strange man who regularly slept in her bed.

'And you've got to stop calling it 'the spare room' in front of my mum' Jet Tea continued.

A small period of silence became sandwiched between the subject of Hayden's drunken sleeping arrangements and the next topic.

'How did it go with that girl last night?' asked Hayden.

'The Scottish girl?' said Jet Tea, feigning nonchalance.

'Was she Scottish? Yeah, her.'

'Yeah, not bad. I got her number.'

Hayden was simultaneously impressed and concerned, and ill, because less than twenty-four hours ago, Jet Tea was in a relationship.

Even less than 24 hours ago, Jet Tea was in his kitchen. It was approximately three in the morning and he'd just carefully dumped Hayden in his sister's bed and gone downstairs for one more beer (Hayden didn't need one). He stumbled into his kitchen and picked up a glass bottle from next to the fridge, silently chiding himself for not putting more bottles in the fridge earlier that day. He flopped into a chair at the kitchen table and opened the unremarkably warm bottle with a bottle-opener he always kept on him. The newly free air hissed from within the glass as the falling bottle cap clinked lightly on the table.

Jet Tea took a sip of warm lager and put the bottle back down. Instantly, he noticed that the bottle stood at the far end of the table, even further than his outstretched arm could reach. With drunken, fractured logic Jet Tea surmised that he must have accidentally slid the bottle across the table when he put it down and had been absurdly lucky in its not carrying on over the edge. He snorted a small giggle at this remarkable fluke and picked the beer up to take another sip, somehow oblivious to the curious fact that it was once again well within reach. Jet Tea sat in deep, grim thought for a few minutes until he stumbled off to bed, leaving the beer unfinished on the kitchen table. Definitely on the kitchen table.

'Have you text her?' Hayden asked, each syllable making the muscles around his brain throb.

'Nah, probably a bit soon, eh?' Jet Tea replied, reaching into his pocket.

'Yeah you're not wrong.'

'She's a nurse, you know' said Jet Tea, staring at his phone.

'Really? Cool' replied Hayden, who was trying

very hard to minimise the number of syllables necessary for a comprehensible answer. Three was the record to beat.

'She lives at the hospital' said Jet Tea, pressing buttons on his phone.

'Lives there?' asked Hayden, smashing his record.

'Yeah, well next to it' Jet Tea corrected himself as he pressed SEND. 'In the staff accommodation. That means she's really near the Treaty as well.'

'Are you going to text her?' asked Hayden, somehow managing to condense the question into two syllables without sacrificing its clarity.

Jet Tea sheepishly returned his mobile phone to his pocket and stared back to the TV with a guilty grin upon his face.

'Oh' said Hayden, winning the syllable game.

Half a mile away, a sleeping Scottish girl was brought back into hungover reality with an irritating 'beep' and the words; *'Hello Im Jet Tea'* staring at her from a bright screen.

'Do you have work tonight?' Jet Tea asked Hayden as they strolled down the stairs into the kitchen in search of slimy hangover food.

'No. Why do you ask?'

'Well,' said Jet Tea as he picked his unfinished beer bottle up off of the floor, 'it's Friday night.'

'Oh yeah' said Hayden, whose job had gradually, over the years, caused him to forget what a weekend was. 'So it is.'

Jet Tea poured warm, flat beer into the sink and put the bottle back on the kitchen table. 'We should go to the treaty.'

'Again? Two nights in a row? Why?'

'Well it might be a good night tonight.'

'You wanted to go into London last night.'

'Yeah I did.'

'Let's do that.'

'I don't know.'

'Why? London's surely even better on a wossname.'

'Friday.'

'Friday.'

'Yeah but I don't feel like it now.'

'You'd rather go to the treaty twice in a row?'

'Yeah.'

'It's not that good there.'

'Yeah but Fridays are alright.'

'It's only one tube.'

'Still. Might have to work Saturday. Tea?'

'No thanks… Oh, right.'

'Oh right?'

'I get it.'

'You get what?'

'You want to bump into wossname.'

'Gemma?'

'Gemma.'

'No I don't.'

'Then how did you know I meant Gemma?'

'I… alright. Please can we go Treaty?'

'Alright.'

'Yay!'

Hayden laughed, and for the first time that "morning" his head didn't hurt. Jet Tea opened the fridge and teamed up bacon with bread, butter, tomato ketchup, a toaster and a frying pan. 'Watch me cook' he boasted.

'Have you heard from Maurice?' asked Jet Tea as they chewed their food.

'No. Why, what did he do?'

Jet Tea suddenly remembered that he alone maintained the memory of their Thursday night. He swallowed his bacon. 'Oh yeah, you must have missed it. He got chucked out.'

Hayden invented a worried laugh. 'Why?' he asked.

'He wanted to hear early Beatles' Jet Tea replied.

'So?'

'He wouldn't take 'no' for an answer.'

'Oh.' Said Hayden as the penny dropped. 'I'm sure he'll turn up.'

Half a mile away, Maurice slowly and shakily lifted his face from the cushion of his living room sofa, like a turtle being born. He turned to face the wall. The words 'I AM A CUNT', in two-foot high letters, took pride of place above the television, scrawled in navy blue felt-tip. Maurice recognised his handwriting.

'Are you alright?' asked Hayden.

'No' said Jet Tea. 'My head is killing me and I've already been sick once.' His phone beeped.

Hayden sighed at Jet Tea's spectacular ability to miss the point. 'I meant about Tara.'

'Who?' asked Jet Tea with an authenticity that Hayden would not have believed in a million years. 'Oh, yeah. That was weeks ago.'

Hayden sat up. 'Mate' he said, 'It was yesterday.'

'Yesterday? Yeah sorry it was' said Jet Tea, staring at his phone with a smile.

Hayden, spectacularly missing the point, sighed at Jet Tea's fake contentment. As skin deep as Hayden steadfastly believed it was, he knew there was little he could do to change the way Jet Tea dealt with trauma. He had been like this once before, and back then, same as in this instance, he'd sat out the ordeal as though it were happening to someone he'd never met.

The phone rang and broke Hayden's train of thought. Jet Tea sat up with a start, and then left the table to answer it, as most would. Hayden ignored the muffled, one sided conversation from the next room as he leant back in his chair waiting for his throbbing brain to stop swimming. Jet Tea returned.

'Can you help me tidy up?' he asked. 'Mum's coming back and she was a bit annoyed with the mess.'

'Yeah, absolutely' Hayden replied. 'I don't suppose me sprawled half naked in the spare room helped her mood either.'

Jet Tea winced at that remark and picked the beer bottle up from the floor again. Something felt a little off about that meagre activity. He poured the beer into the sink and put the bottle by the far wall of the kitchen, next to the other recyclables. He froze there for a second and stared at nothing, which is an entirely difficult thing to achieve if you try it. If you don't try it it's the easiest thing in the world. Jet Tea wasn't trying. Several seconds passed.

'Mate' Hayden called as he turned the tap on.

Several more seconds passed. The significance of a length of time constantly alters to suit the activity that is enduring that time. A minute's silence may as well be an eternity to an indifferent schoolchild, yet to the very same child, a half hour playtime session is no time at all. There is a good reason for this and all other possible examples; time has a terrible sense of humour.

So, as it is, thirty-odd seconds of staring into space, especially when not alone, is a long time.

'Jet Tea' Hayden shouted. Jet Tea's trance broke.

'Eh?'

'You alright mate?' asked Hayden.

Jet Tea shuddered. 'Where was that beer bottle?' he asked.

Hayden made no effort to understand what his friend was talking about. 'Sorry?'

All of a sudden, Jet Tea forgot where he was going with this. All felt normal. Then he received another text from Gemma. It read *'Good, thanks x'* and he smiled.

The early evening sky turned ever so gradually more navy blue. Maurice trod with caution as the grey brickwork of the Treaty loomed. He was sure he had done something naughty the previous night, but his friends had not told him yet. Receiving retroactive correspondent reports regarding your own day-to-day life can be rather distressing, yet to the more headstrong and confident drinker, they eventually serve to build character, especially with increasing frequency. Maurice had long since stumbled drunkenly over that hurdle. Having Jet Tea and Hayden tell him what he'd been up to on a night out had become his personal equivalent to reading the morning paper. Also, it can't have been any worse than Hayden's comment about kicking black kids to death. It is immature to say that being drunk is no excuse for poor behaviour; of course it is. Human beings are imperfect, and alcohol merely highlights that.

They walked through the door to the sound of *Help* by The Beatles and Maurice experienced a brief chill of déjà vu. Then the three of them took a deep breath, huddled together and pushed for the bar.

The Treaty on a Friday is a far different experience to the Treaty on any other night of the week. A table is unlikely to be found and is unanticipated among the regulars. Drinks are served strictly in plastic cups, which most sensibly assume is to prevent injury (except for the older clientele who strongly believe it is enforced to annoy them out of the door and make way for the younger crowd), and the ten-a-penny indie dance songs that the customers have convinced themselves they like are blasted out considerably louder than usual, in order to eliminate conversation and increase drinking. Local wisdom implores visitors to spend a drunken Friday night at the Treaty, then go there for an afternoon pint on a Saturday and see if they realise it's the same pub they were in the night before, throwing up to old Razorlight songs. The staff really are marvelous at cleaning up.

Maurice stood eagerly behind a large man with a shaved head and a white short-sleeved shirt that was a bit too small for him. He had been ordering drinks for quite some time and kept amending his order every time one of his loud, wobbly friends stumbled past.

'-And a sambucca' the big man shouted at the flustered bartender. 'Sorry, TWO sambuccas. Four.

Craig! Oi, Craig! 'Boo-cah? 'Boo-cah! Wanna 'boo-cah you dozy prick? He can't hear. Let's 'ave six. Fuck it. Wossthis? Nah I didn't order this. I said PINT. Oh, 'ere he is. Craig! Whaddayawant? Snakebite as well. Nah I reckon that's it. Cheers. And a J.D.'

Eventually the bartender (who was, fortunately, fluent) completed the taxing drink order and Maurice, by now bouncing up and down with impatience, was next. The bartender instantly recognised him and held his hands up, as though in defence.

'Mate they're playing Beatles' he said with alarm.

Maurice was confused. 'What? I just want a drink' he replied.

The bartender took a deep breath and nodded.

Elsewhere, Jet Tea was eagerly marching to and fro amidst the hot, bumpy crowd, wiggling his fingers excitedly and jolting his head from side to side in an attempt to locate Gemma.

He thought he spied the back of a blonde head leave the room toward the beer garden and gasped embarrassingly. Fortunately the music was so loud that nobody heard. When the possible Gemma had completely disappeared he pounced into a short jog through the pub to catch up with her. It was cut short by a powerful collision with the sweaty, outstretched arm of a large man and the next half-second was obscured by an almighty downpour of lager over Jet Tea's face. An unfortunate outcome of the collision.

Jet Tea blinked with alarm and looked up. There, he found the furious stare of a man recently bereaved of his pint.

'You prick' exclaimed the man, loudly.

'Sorry' said Jet Tea with partial disinterest as he attempted, unsuccessfully, to sidestep his new adversary.

'You spilt my pint' continued the man, angrily.

Jet Tea wiped the beer from his face and looked about the gentleman. His arm was outstretched among the crowd and had been when the collision occurred.

'Sorry' he said again, 'but you did have your arm out mate.'

The man screwed his face up at this.

'What?'

'Well' said Jet Tea, 'it's well busy in here and you're waving your arms about. It was bound to happen.' He had adopted his slightly exaggerated cockney tone when saying this.

'Fuck you. Are you gonna get me another one?'

The man's arm remained outstretched. Whereas

before the arm was likely positioned so as part of a dance routine, it was now spread in a threatening manner, accentuating his superior stature over Jet Tea.

'I don't think so' he said, defiantly. 'I can't afford it. My mum stopped giving me pocket money because I kept knocking people's drinks over.'

'Don't try and be funny with me, you prick' the man shouted back. At least he recognised the attempt at humour, thought Jet Tea.

He wasn't sure why he was being so brave in the face of spilt beer, given his size and (for the time being) sobriety, but either way, he now realised that if his new foe wanted to hurt him, he would have done so already. He continued to prod the beast.

'It was your fault' he shouted. 'You can't go around with your arms out like a bull in a candy store. And look, you're still doing it.'

The man would not lower his arm. He continued to try and intimidate Jet Tea with his wingspan, clutching a near-empty plastic pint cup.

'Buy me a new one' he said.

'If I knock your beer over again and it's my fault I promise I will buy you a pint and a new hat' replied Jet Tea, before ducking under the arm and darting outside, followed only by the begrudging gaze of his victim.

He stood in the doorway of the beer garden, trying to see through the smoky crowd to find Gemma. Time was, before the introduction of the smoking ban in pubs, one would go outside to get fresh air. Nowadays we're all more likely to breath comfortably inside a pub than out. He spotted Maurice, strolling around clutching three plastic pints, trying in vain not to spill bits of them over his fingers. Maurice spotted Jet Tea.

'Jet Tea!' he cried, proving that he'd seen him.

They headed over to each other, meeting half way.

'Take your pint' said Maurice, 'Christ knows where Hayden is.'

'Cheers' said Jet Tea, relieving Maurice of his duty. They sipped simultaneously for a moment.

'I haven't seen Gemma yet' said Jet Tea, deliberately initiating a conversation.

'Who?'

'That girl I met last night. I've been texting her all day.'

Maurice nodded. He remembered very little about the previous night, although he did hold vague recollections of his friend spending a lot of time with an attractive girl with blonde hair and a stripy scarf. He was sure he'd seen her this evening as well.

'How did it go?' asked Maurice, who was less taken aback by Jet Tea's rapid rebound than Hayden had been earlier that day.

'Well' Jet Tea started, before slipping dreamily into some kind of light-headed trance as he beheld the flowing crowd ahead of him, obscured by both smoke and his own absent mind. He observed himself having the conversation with Maurice and, although surprised by his own responses, he remained a silent, unobtrusive observer.

'She wants me' replied Jet Tea. 'I can tell.'

Maurice was impressed, although for some nagging reason not entirely convinced. 'She wants you? Nice work mate.'

'Yeah she does.'

'How do you feel?' asked Maurice.

'Yeah, she seems interesting' Jet Tea replied, still keenly watching the crowd in hope of spotting her. 'Either way.'

Jet Tea's fractured string of indifferent-sounding stock remarks continued. 'You know how it is.' They began to irritate Maurice.

'Mate' said Maurice. 'You sound like you're not that bothered about her.'

'Yeah' Jet Tea sighed. 'I can take it or leave it, you know.'

'Then how come you've been running around for the last half an hour looking for her?'

'I'm not looking for her' Jet Tea replied so quickly that it leads one to wonder whether he may have been anticipating that question all along. He took another sip.

'She's nice' he said. 'I don't know if I'm that into her.'

Maurice rolled his eyes up to the sky in frustration. He suddenly remembered why he wasn't convinced by his friend's claims that Gemma wanted him more than he wanted her.

'Yet you've been texting her all day?'

'Yeah, well since I got up anyway' said Jet Tea. Maurice didn't understand how that didn't constitute 'all day'.

'And has she been texting you as much? How many times?'

'Huh? Oh, two or three. She said she was going to be here.'

'Did you ask her that or did she just happen to let you know?'

'Oh yeah, I asked her.'

'What else did she say? Who initiated the texting?'

'I did.'

'What did you say?'

'Huh? "Hi it's me Jet Tea from last night" or something, I can't remember. Why?'

'No reason. What did she say?'

'She said that yeah she remembers me.'

'Then what?'

'She put a kiss at the end of her text.'

'So?'

'Well that means something, doesn't it?'

'Mate, all girls put a kiss at the end. It's preprogrammed in them.'

'Nah, I don't think it is.'

'My nan puts a kiss at the end of her texts to her book club mates. It means nothing, trust me.'

'Yeah, yeah it does. She's in love with me. I don't put kisses at the end of texts to men.'

'Men and women are different, though' replied Maurice.

'They're not that different.'

'Really?' he asked. 'And how long does it take your mum to grow a beard?'

Jet Tea laughed it off. Maurice groaned loudly

with irritation, gulped down the last of his beer and placed Hayden's unclaimed pint abruptly on the floor. He grabbed his infuriating friend by the shoulders.

'Listen, mate' he cried. 'You're not thinking straight. This sort of attitude will get worse if you don't start realising how fucking moronic you're sounding. You broke up with Tara yesterday. This is a severe rebound and if you don't address it you're going to start thinking you're James fucking Bond or something. Mark my words, Jet Tea; this girl is not in love with you. Stop trying to project your rebound obsessions onto someone else. It doesn't do you any fucking favours. It just makes you look like a cunt. Nobody's buying it.'

Jet Tea was shaken. He had no idea what Maurice meant. As far as he was concerned, Gemma quite honestly did love him. Did she? Jet Tea briefly thought he felt something tiny and far, far away at the bottom left-hand corner of his mind that may have meekly whispered a possible 'she might not.'

He shrugged. 'I'm pretty sure she wants me.'

Maurice cried out again and grabbed Jet Tea by the arm.

'Right' he said. 'Come with me.'

He led Jet Tea, almost dragging him, through the beer garden, past the huddled crowd of smokers and out through a gate at the side. Jet Tea was vaguely curious as to where they were going but mainly unnerved at the whole affair.

The side gate led to a secluded area behind the pub. It was a car park, as unfrequented and desolate as pub car parks often (and most sensibly) are. Except it wasn't completely unfrequented. Across the bare concrete, leant against the wall of the pub and not completely hidden by the night, stood two bodies, huddled together in a passionate embrace. Their faces were pressed tightly together and their arms explored each other's backs vigorously.

Jet Tea recognised the stripy scarf and blonde hair of one of them with no difficulty. It was Gemma, perpetually locked in an enthusiastic kiss with a tall, smartly dressed man with good hair and a well-toned face.

Maurice felt slightly bad for what he was putting his friend through, but he would not deny himself the greater purpose of their little excursion to the car park.

'See what I mean now?' he asked, before disappearing back toward the pub in search of beer and Beatles songs.

Jet Tea nodded, to nobody, and briefly pondered

waiting for Gemma to notice him. He decided against it and fought off the pull of an ensuing frown, finished his beer and headed back to the warmth to catch up with his friends.

Jet Tea Buys CDs

Time, which had been a conniving and detestable little bugger of late, played the wholly unfunny prank of dragging yesterday's morning back in on Jet Tea, but twisting it ever so slightly in a gruesome way. Though it would be somewhat economical, it would also be unnecessary to fully go through all the tropes of that morning in any detail yet again, being as they are so fresh in recent memory.

Jet Tea awoke. His head hurt. Hayden was asleep in his absent sister's room. They stumbled downstairs. They had breakfast. They left the building.

The differences were in the aforementioned gruesome twists. Jet Tea's hangover was now not cushioned by vague memories of a fruitful night. He remembered seeing Gemma, the girl he'd been searching for without admittance all night, glued to the face of someone who was irritatingly not he. He also sketchily recalled storming back into the pub, shouting a nasty word at the DJ, slipping and falling in an oddly familiar beer puddle and eventually hobbling out with a wet backside, fervently grumbling the phrase 'she wants me' (and variations thereupon) all the way home.

After collapsing into bed with all the grace of a building demolition, Jet Tea was then woken by a phone call from Hayden, who was waiting outside his house stepping hither and thither, attempting to lean on thin air and uttering noises that were halfway between a breath and a sentence. Jet Tea let him in and found him either concerned for his friend or unwilling to brave a bus ride home. A conclusion was never reached.

He dreamed about Gemma, that night. A short while after his and Hayden's slurred conversation gradually became mutual snoring, Jet Tea's world turned vast and empty. He looked about himself and saw only his bed, which he was suddenly not in (in fact he was a good half a minute's walk away from it), and pale grey. He could not figure out if he was indoors or outdoors because the shade of grey surrounding him was one that would suit either wall or dreary sky.

Jet Tea wiped his brow and imagined Gemma and as he did so, as if with the flick of his hand upon his forehead, she came into being, a reasonable distance from him (much further from his bed than he was). Was this lucid dreaming or simply dreaming about an environment that could be controlled? The word 'dream' never actually came up.

Gemma seemed to be walking away from Jet Tea, though she was not gaining any distance. Was he also moving? She was crying, by the looks of it. Crying and walking. Walking home? She was dressed in the same clothes she wore at the Treaty when Jet Tea saw her with that man. Had he done something to upset her? Maybe this would serve to increase her interest in Jet Tea.

The surrounding grey dimmed ahead. Something vast and intimidating rose up ahead of Gemma. It silhouetted and completely dwarfed her, although it seemed more interested in Jet Tea.

A strained sound quavered and groaned all about the place, a voice coming from everywhere, coming into being.

'The sky is never grey' it hissed. 'It is, at worst, only shielded by grey.'

Then a massive coffee table hurtled rapidly toward Jet Tea's face.

Jet Tea awoke in discomfort, drenched in a cold sweat (hopefully). The familiar morning proceeded to happen.

After dropping Hayden back home, Jet Tea decided against going back to bed. Instead he drove into the town center, parked his car on the high street and went for a walk.

The intense early afternoon sunlight, piercing his eyes and hangover, was rather soothing to Jet Tea. As he strolled intrepidly through the busy high street, glaring through the wallpaper of familiar chain stores and blurred groups of podgy families clutching myriad plastic bags, he began to feel good. He bobbed his head fluidly as he stepped, like a bold pigeon, and began wiggling his fingers with his step, which itself had become so pronounced as to almost being a kind of walking dance.

The big sun, perpetually looming and radiating his ill-chosen black t-shirt, reminded Jet Tea of the vast, ominous, shadowy thing in his dream. He could never gain any proximity to it, much like the sun. It almost seemed to be looking at him despite its facelessness, much like the sun. And in spite of its vast size and clear, dangerous power, it was nonetheless comforting and safe, much like the sun. Jet Tea continued his faux dance-walk through the high street, bopping his head from side to side and wiggling his fingers avidly, until the approaching pink glow of the letters H, M and V came into view.

At that moment Jet Tea made a snap decision to get into music more. He had had enough of Maurice and Hayden's musical jargon conversations while he silently sipped beer in the shadows. Next time they met, Jet Tea would be the expert on alternative music while they listened in awe. No more spending extra money on lager because his lack of vocal contribution meant he would drink quicker. No more waiting for someone to mention food so he could finally chime in with his expertise. No more saying 'my friends are into that' and leaving the conversation there when he met a girl. *When he met a girl.* Of course. It had to be done.

He marched into HMV and set a course for the aisle named 'rock and pop'. He didn't have much of a plan, but he had money and vague recollections of Maurice and Hayden's past discussions.

Stalking the aisles of rock and pop obscurity, Jet Tea occasionally glimpsed band names that looked familiar, even though he couldn't quite read all of them. The shapes and lengths of some of the words corresponded to the sound of the words when his friends had said them in the past.

Finally a particular CD stood out. Partially hidden behind the overlapping CDs in front of it sat a shiny plastic case on which sat a haloed but slightly nervous looking ape-like creature, most likely a monkey, boxed in a crude, square chart and surrounded by a plethora of randomly placed numbers and shapes. The CD cover was mainly brown and white but even so gave the impression of being colourful and exciting.

Something about the CD cover, the wide-eyed little innocent primate trapped in such a mundane shape while a bonkers shindig of surrealism happens around him, really appealed to Jet Tea and, as he approached it with an enthusiastic thirst, he spied a familiar word on the right hand side of the case. 'PIXIES'. He knew the name 'PIXIES'. He'd heard Maurice talk about 'PIXIES' often. That settled it. The wonderful CD cover, the fact that it was a band his friends liked. This 'PIXIES' was to be Jet Tea's first musical purchase. He took the one he liked, which was called *Doolittle* (a word Jet Tea envisioned himself making up during an excited turn) and several others that were behind it so he could begin to 'properly get into' the band, then marched on to find more music.

The tactic of picking up CDs by bands he'd heard his friends mention ended up working quite well for Jet Tea, who left HMV with a kaleidoscope of records by bands called 'Blur', 'The Vaselines', 'Joy Division' and 'The Smiths.' As an added bonus, on the way to the counter he passed the t-shirt section of the shop and noticed the 'PIXIES *Doolittle*' album cover on a t-shirt. Jet Tea picked that up as well. He was sure Maurice and Hayden were fond of all these bands and as such they would hardly fail to appeal to him. If ever there were something on this planet that would divide Jet Tea and his friends, music would surely not be it. He danced eagerly back to his car and ventured home to begin a brand new hobby. Things were going to change.

A Special Delivery

The air was crisp, the sky was bright and fair in a way only the early morning of an exciting day can be. Jet Tea leant on his car door, clutching a small parcel and wiggling the fingers of his free hand with promise and trepidation. He beheld in front of him three identical rows of tall, red-bricked buildings boasting a multitude of square windows and secure, heavy doors. Across the road there stood a hospital, and these buildings accommodated the hospital's staff.

The glum but romantic rolling bass and clockwork drumming of Joy Division thundered from within his vehicle as Jet Tea mulled over his plan. He looked at the parcel; 'JEMMA' was written on it in his best handwriting. He'd been lucky enough to find a posh pen among all the biros that one inevitably accumulates throughout life. He pondered that. Life is, ultimately, the involuntary acquisition of an inexhaustible supply of cheap ball-point pens. Occasionally one may stumble upon a refillable chrome parker and such instances must be cherished. He would not add her address, assuming he would be fortunate to find out what it was. Jet Tea liked imagining the ambiguous notion on Gemma's part that he must have been to her door personally. He thought it romantic for her to believe that.

The item within was Jet Tea's own personal copy of *1984*. He felt Gemma deserved it more than he. Now was the time to part with it and he suffered no materialistic sense of loss, only an indomitable, immaterial gain with its departure. There was no time to lose, this was the moment.

Before long, the front door to one of the blocks opened and a young man emerged. He looked in a hurry as he bounded out of the building toward the hospital, but more crucially, toward Jet Tea's car.

'Mate' Jet Tea shouted.

The man shot a meagre glance partially in the direction of the address but remained uncertain as he continued.

'Mate' Jet Tea shouted again. The man stopped, but did not look very pleased about doing so.

'Yes?' he replied.

'Can you tell me where Gemma lives?'

The man frowned. 'Gemma who?' he asked.

Jet Tea realised he did not know the answer to that. 'Erm, Scottish Gemma?'

His would-be helper, bereft of sufficient data, huffed. 'There are several hundred people living here' he said, condescendingly. 'I can't help you mate. Sorry' he didn't sound sorry. 'And turn that fucking music down' he continued. 'There are doctors and nurses on call that need to sleep.'

Jet Tea ignored the last part of that exchange. All that mattered to him was that he rectified the first part. The man had begun walking again. Jet Tea was frantic. 'She has blonde hair and a stripy scarf' he yelled. The man stopped again and, without looking back at his verbal assailant, sighed.

'I've seen a blonde girl with a stripy scarf going in and out of there' he said, pointing to the same building from which he emerged. 'I think she has an accent.' With that he darted off quicker than ever.

'Cheers' shouted Jet Tea. There was no reply, but he didn't care. He had the information he needed, but he'd also, thanks to the conversation, become aware of a blatant oversight; there could be any number of Gemmas living in that building, he had to be more specific with his address. He pulled a biro from his jeans pocket and scribbled 'SCOTSH ONE' beneath her name. Finally he sprinted over to the door and slid the parcel through the communal post box. The deed was done.

Jet Tea spent the next few days in a blissful trance as he replayed his incredible deed over and over again in his mind. He retained just enough awareness and basic functions to get through day-to-day life, but all that really just simpered by as he thought of how he'd almost definitely captured Gemma's attention once again. He knew she was head over heels in love with him, now she'd perhaps work out that he in turn felt something for her. It wasn't much, but it was enough.

Of course, all of this newfound positivity was largely thanks to his recent discovery of music. How had he sat by so many times, completely extraneous to his friends' enthusiastic discussions, arguments and drunken mutterings about a topic he'd -until recently- thought to be trivial and uninteresting? Those last few days, molding and shaping his emotions to fit whatever lilting, romantic or bittersweet distorted pop song would soundtrack that particular moment, the incongruous pleasure of bleak Joy Division underplaying his passionate excitement or happy, bouncy Pixies complimenting moments of near-despair as what he'd briefly mistake for reality would cloud over his mind like a raincloud on a bank holiday. Those last few days were a musical revelation.

Jet Tea's mother and sister noticed how his bedroom, until now perpetually silent (save for those unfortunate instances in which he and Tara had not waited for them to leave the house), had become a constantly intrusive soundtrack to their mundane indoor activities. Imagine the darkly comic majesty of *There Goes My Gun* while looking for your shoes, or the beautiful yet retroactively foreboding thunder of *Atmosphere* while frying an egg. Jet Tea's family didn't have to.

As the weeks passed, Jet Tea began to notice how some music made him angry. Songs that didn't seem to fit among the ones he loved were an annoyance to him. They didn't belong, and he wondered what they were doing there, whether he'd accidentally pause his channel-surfing on a pop music network whoring out its latest chart-darling again and again to ensure that absolutely nobody misses it, or being over-ruled as to which radio station his team would listen to at work, Jet Tea discovered that some music was not fun, not for him and did not fill him with the same wonder, optimism and romance that his chosen bands did.

One evening, work was abnormally quiet. Jet Tea's temporary position in the school cafeteria had come to an end and he was now in his second week as a chef in a modest little English pub, selling traditional food and resisting the urge to challenge his abilities. Being in a kitchen which, for all the available access to the outside world they enjoyed may as well have been a submarine, Jet Tea and his colleagues were naturally unaware that there was a fully-fledged rain and thunderstorm raging outside that was most likely discouraging nearby residents from eating out. Either way, all that mattered to them was that they could close early, this meant they'd each acquired several hours that they'd previously considered lost. Until time travel would be invented, this was the next best thing.

Naturally, the unanimous decision was to get to the pub as soon as possible and drink until the hours ran dry. Once the last surface was wiped and the last errant chip was swept away, they left the kitchen and changed out of their whites.

Jet Tea pulled his Pixies T-shirt from his locker

and over his skinny body. His head chef Joe, a large, rough-skinned bulldog of a man who was likely often referred to as a 'bloke' looked over and grinned.

'Not that fucking T-shirt again' he laughed, raising his bald head up to gather attention. 'Look at Jet Tea!'

Jet Tea shivered momentarily, but that was as embarrassed as he'd get. Glen, a weasel-esque nineteen year old who had too much hair gel and not enough spinal bones, looked over and sniggered. 'Do you wash that thing?' he asked. Jet Tea giggled. 'Get over it mate' he said. 'I don't wash my willy either. Do you want to gawp at that as well?'

Joe and Glen laughed. Whilst Jet Tea was not, by societal standards, 'one of them', they always had ample time for his geeky, accidental wit and enthusiasm for being mildly bullied. As such they never neglected to invite him out with them, even though he seldom obliged.

They arrived at the nearest pub, The Good Yarn; a stoic, ugly place with few windows and a deliberate, stifling darkness that discourages the lonely daytime drinkers from getting out of their seats and leaving. As they approached the bar Joe stopped and pointed at a solitary figure on a barstool, staring into his half-finished pint of ale. He had a frizzy mane of dark facial hair and wore a long, tattered grey jacket. Joe smirked.

'Check out Gandalf' he said to the others, who laughed. He then turned to Jet Tea and said 'Oi, Harry Potter, go and see your mate Gandalf. Look, he's lonely! Go and say hello' he nudged Jet Tea with his elbow. 'Go on Harry!'

'Yeah?' he replied defiantly. 'How many evil wizards have you defeated?'

'What?' asked Joe.

'Exactly. You do the maths.'

Jet Tea snorted a meek chuckle and said no more. Gandalf, who had clearly heard Joe's remarks, looked around, an annoyed sadness in his small eyes. He looked away. As the colleagues continued to approach the bar he looked again, this time at Jet Tea. At that Gandalf stood up and promptly left the pub, without finishing his drink.

'Whoops, hit a nerve there mate' said Glen.

As they sat around a small table glugging their lagers and, amidst loud musings on football and tabloid politics Jet Tea began to remember why he rarely spent time with his colleagues outside of work, he took out his phone.

'Fucking page three' moaned Joe, staring at a newspaper. 'No tits today. It's the only reason I buy it.'

Jet Tea looked up from his phone. 'Don't you have the internet?' he asked.

'Nah, don't trust the internet, me' replied Joe, throwing the paper aside. 'Too many perverts.'

Jet Tea shrugged and went back to his phone screen. There was no message from Gemma. Still. Two weeks had passed by since the special delivery. Surely she'd have received the book by now? Why would somebody receive a gift from someone they loved and not acknowledge it? For the first time in a long while, Jet Tea felt a frown form on his face. He clenched the phone in his rigid fist, tighter and tighter as the ugly sounds of his drunken co-workers further irritated him. A crap song that sounded like it was made rather than born lingered with too much treble from the pub's rubbish sound system and Jet Tea began to feel itchy. He continued to squeeze his phone, wanting it to crumble in his grip. As the clashing sounds of the annoying song and the annoying conversation seemed to grow louder and fill his head as well as his ears he found himself grinding his teeth. A niggling feeling that he wanted to turn to sedimentary rock and crumble away permanently began to overtake him. Then, as the sounds distorted and amplified and they were no longer a bad discussion and bad music, but simply bad sound, he did just that. His vision distorted and everything turned translucent grey, then just grey with no definition. Everything was suddenly silent, but that only lasted a second. Then the sound of his name cut through the stony silence and he crumbled into fragments of clay.

Or so he thought. Joe had addressed him, brought him back to life. The song was once again just irritating and in the background. The boring conversation had stopped.

'We're gonna head off' said Joe. 'You coming?'

He dropped his phone onto the table. 'Yeah' he replied. 'Just popping outside for a moment.'

Jet Tea stood outside at the front of the pub. He needed fresh air, which was unfortunately in short supply in this section of West London. He took a deep breath and looked up to the sky; clouds shrouded the entire thing. Grey-black clouds that managed to make the night even darker. This upset Jet-Tea and he began to sulk, standing on his own on a dull, wet street waiting to say goodbye to people he didn't even like.

But then something occurred to him. '*The sky is never grey*', someone had said recently. He didn't really think much about it, or even fully understand it, but he felt that it was helping now. He sent Gemma a text, it read; *Hop ur well*. Then he smiled. Gemma may not have been in touch lately, but he was sure she had a valid reason that had nothing to do with the things Maurice had said on the night of the spilled drink.

'Jet Tea' said a voice from behind him. He turned around, there was Joe. 'You alright?'

He smiled again. 'Yes' he replied. 'Sorry about that. Where's Glen?'

'Just getting his car' said Joe. 'He only had one drink, don't worry. Want a lift?'

'Alright.'

Before long Glen's car pulled up beside them. A familiar song was pulsating from within. Jet Tea recognised it; it was *Yuko and Hiro* by Blur, one of his favourites from the album *The Great Escape*. He entered the car with a huge, satisfied grin on his face. Perhaps these people were a bit more like him than he'd assumed. In the twilight of the car's interior he gazed upon Joe and Glen with a newfound respect. These people, who altruistically mask their intelligence and integrity behind the necessary façade of their masculine duty. They heroically suppress their passions in order to live comfortably alongside their Page 3-oggling, lager-guzzling, football-worshiping kinsmen who must have their expectations satiated, but here they are letting someone in to observe their true selves. The masks have slipped. Perhaps these people truly are friends.

Joe snorted; 'fuck that shit off' and Glen changed the radio station with a chuckle. An ugly-sounding song, not unlike the one playing in the pub moments ago, replaced Blur.

Jet Tea's jaw fell in disappointed shock. 'What?'

'You like that shit do you?' laughed Glen.

'That's Blur!' said Jet Tea, aghast. '*The Great Escape* is one of the greatest albums of the nineties.'

Joe and Glen burst into laughter. 'The nineties!' repeated Joe. 'Get you retro!'

Jet Tea didn't know what that meant, but nonetheless he stood his ground. 'You know nothing' he cried, trying his best to ape Maurice. 'You know nothing about proper music. You would never listen to Joy Division or The Vaselines, because you're stuck in this boring trap, listening to shit you think you like because you're too scared or lazy to search deeper.'

Joe stopped laughing. 'Don't call me boring mate' he said sternly. 'Don't forget who pays your wages.'

Jet Tea opened the car door. 'Forget it' he said with a huff.

'Are you going to walk home because the designated driver doesn't like Blur?' asked Glen with disbelief. 'Get over yourself!'

Jet Tea said no more as he shut the car door behind him and began his long walk home. He was right, and despite having only really been into music for a couple of weeks, he knew he was right. They were boring, everyone was boring. It's rather easy to notice a change in others that isn't actually happening when you yourself are changing and not realising it. This town was growing increasingly more boring.

The Five Pence Carrier Bag

For the first time in a long while, Maurice was awake and active at nine in the morning. Of course, he had been out drinking the night before and was still a little the worse for wear on this day, but every once in a while mercy would grant him a milder hangover, alongside vaguely fond memories of the preceding evening and as such, a rather calm, reflective mood with which to treat his sore head.

There had been no intoxicated bellowing at despicable hostiles. No empty, unintelligible threats to DJs who would steadfastly refuse to bend the night's soundtrack to his stubborn will. Nothing of the sort. Instead, Maurice largely recalled splendid conversation, good music and welcome attention from a young lady called Fiona with short red hair and a tattoo of a lemming on her neck. She was Slovakian and thus spoke English beautifully, because she'd learnt it properly in a school rather than picked it up from idiots. He couldn't quite remember where he was or who he was with so he fretted mildly about never seeing Fiona again, but the present memories were enough to placate him.

After pottering about his kitchen for a few minutes with no clear aim in mind, Maurice took his lukewarm coffee into his spare bedroom, which he'd recently disassembled to the best of his ability in order to set up a makeshift recording studio. The mattress was upturned and propped to the wall by a couple of idle microphone stands, his desktop computer had seemingly grown several large, metallic limbs adorned with knobs and dials and a tambourine unintentionally acted as a temporary doorstop.

He decided now was as good a time as any to record the last few lyrics to a song that was giving him grief in the recording stages. He was uncertain of the correct tone and pitch in which to deliver a certain line, and hoped that in his relatively productive state of mind he could accomplish it, so he pulled a piano stool up to his desk, booted up the recording software, loaded the track to record and darted over to the microphone stands.

He sang;

'The sun is not rewarding, it's just glare
The rain is not depressing, it's always there'

Grimacing with discontent, he leapt back over to the computer to cease the recording and then tried again. Still imperfect. Perhaps if he went into it from the previous couplet, which he was confident with and would happily re-record, it might be better;

'Your tie is not impressing, take it off and breathe
Or if your high horse permits it, saddle up and leave'

It didn't work. He abandoned that idea and went back to focusing only on the lines that were hassling him. At one point he thought he had it, but his phone rang. It was Jet Tea. Maurice listened loyally as his friend ranted about how his workmates didn't like Blur, and how everyone is boring. He didn't sound quite himself; when exactly did Jet Tea become a music Nazi? Either way, it would have to wait. This song had to be defeated or it would consume him. Maurice politely made Jet Tea aware of his preoccupation and ended the call.

However, the phone call had done it. He could no longer expunge all external irritations and focus solely on this lyric. It was a lost cause, today at least. With a sigh, Maurice shut down his computer and left the chamber of disappointment.

He stalked the ground floor rooms aimlessly for half an hour or so more then decided to put on his shoes and go for a walk. It was a nice day; the rain had stopped in the middle of the night and, despite the majority of his hometown being somewhat humdrum in appearance, there were some visibly pleasing, early Georgian backstreets around the park behind his house. He'd go there, seep into a dreamy state and imagine he was a romantic vagrant in a late nineteenth century gothic novel, his long hair and coat billowing attractively in the soft, melancholy breeze as he gazed wistfully into the ethereal end-point of an aimless journey. That should do it.

It was a pleasant walk, and at the very least Maurice was achieving what he had left his house to achieve. All the irritations of his unfinished work and Jet Tea's intrusive phone call had withered away; even his hangover was more or less gone. He daydreamed about bumping romantically into Fiona again and took in the fresh smelling air of a morning after a storm, old, red-bricked semi-detached houses, distant birdsong and tree branches softly rustling in the modest wind. Eventually he came to the park. Other than a rusty basketball net adorned with cracked blue paint and the obligatory, graffiti-clad park-keeper's shed, it boasted a simple beauty in keeping with the anachronistically rural lanes that ran off of it.

As he approached the furthest corner from where he entered, a pretty little stream came into view. Maurice knew it well, having lived in the area since early childhood. At the bottom of it stood a life-sized sculpture of Christ upon the cross, a memorial that he had curiously never bothered to read. As he'd advanced in years, Maurice's tolerance for unfulfilled curiosity had dwindled, so he decided to finally approach it. During childhood, Maurice had convinced himself that the memorial was, in actuality, the true cross in its original place (correct Biblical geography wasn't very prevalent at so young an age), with the bronze Christ that hung from it serving in place of the man's actual corpse which had long since gone off to heaven. He laughed fondly as he recalled this. Since then, he'd come to believe that, if there was a God, then he must have made the planets in his image (including Pluto; who were we to decide Pluto doesn't belong, just because it's a bit different?) and not man, who must have been the work of the devil instead. The Earth is beautiful and it came first. Why would God then send another creation? If he was all powerful he would have seen the Earth's ravaging coming and decided against it. Plus mankind is ugly. Well, most of it. Maurice bent over to read the slightly faded words that had been engraved on the memorial's podium;

In Loving Memory of the Brave Soldiers Who Fell in

Maurice squinted with confusion. Who 'fell in' what? The stream? What an odd thing to build a memorial to, he thought. How many soldiers had fallen in that stream? Enough to warrant a memorial, it would appear. But surely they hadn't all drowned, had they? Maurice himself had jumped in and out of that very stream countless times growing up. The water barely reached his knees as a six year old. What sort of soldiers were the army recruiting in those days that would face down their mortality in a shallow stream and find defeat? Alternatively, if they had all survived their respective falls, why build a memorial at all? It seems a bit of a tenuous tribute given all of the other atrocities of war. Would the surviving soldiers themselves visit that memorial on occasion and feel moved at the memory of their clumsy slip into the neighbouring water? In fact, what were so many soldiers doing in this park during the war? And so close to the water? It's a miracle we even won if old squaddies were so prolific in being unable to avoid a fatal tumble into a man-made pond, thought Maurice.

He looked again and noticed what he hadn't before. Under the faded tribute was a set of even more faded, near-invisible numbers. Maurice squinted at the engraving;

In Loving Memory of the Brave Soldiers Who Fell in
1914-1918 and 1939-1945

Suddenly the memorial made a lot more sense. With a shrug to himself he carried on walking. He'd been awake for a couple of hours now, and was feeling hungry. Leaving the old, green, leafy suburb behind him he decided to take a detour toward the dreary, austere high street. He fancied a nice sandwich from the posh supermarket, as opposed to the bland, one-pound-fifty egg or cheese affair he was accustomed to. Why shouldn't he treat himself? He may not have as much money as the well-groomed, professional men and women that the posh supermarket had marketed itself towards, but he could at least afford a decent lunch from there, perhaps something with mozzarella and basil instead of cheddar and onion.

It was lunchtime now, and it was a weekday. Therefore the posh supermarket was littered with tall, middle-aged men in grey shirts and blue ties rushing irritably up and down the aisles in meagre attempts to waste as little of their one hour lunch break in a supermarket queue as possible. Not petty enough to feel out of place, Maurice strolled breezily into the shop. He made a bee line for the food section and quickly found what he wanted; an appetising-looking baguette struggling to hold in spinach and sundried tomatoes, clad in cellophane and brown paper. It cost a bit extra than what he was comfortable with, but Maurice didn't mind. He imagined the scornful glares of the richer customers, wondering what this anomaly of a man was doing purchasing food in their supermarket, with his overgrown hair and lack of tie, and it made him smile. He took his sandwich, paired it with a small bottle of orange juice and a bag of posh crisps and headed over to the self-service checkout. They were usually more friendly than the human employees anyway, or at least more conversational.

After he'd scanned his items through to the pleasant, artificial tones of the robotic checkout girl (Maurice had always imagined her to be quite attractive; well-spoken but not elitist, slender but naturally authoritarian, long dark hair draped seductively over one eye), he was asked if he'd like to purchase one or more carrier bags at five pence each. This threw him slightly. He did not frequent the posh supermarket often and had been unaware that they'd taken to charging for their carrier bags. Nevertheless, there was no way a faceless, immobile machine could stop him from taking one. He applauded its reliance on the honesty of strangers but decided his lunch was expensive enough and took one without paying.

On his stroll back home, Maurice took his renewed sense of calm and contentedness with glee and imagined destroying that irritating vocal with swiftness and ease. He'd enjoy his expensive lunch then justify treating himself with a hard afternoon's successful recording.

'Excuse me' called a voice from behind him. Maurice stopped and turned to see a rather large man in a white shirt and black tie creeping up from the entrance to the posh supermarket.

'Yes?' Maurice called back. 'What?'

'Come here please' said the man.

This was slightly unsettling. Who was this authoritarian chap and why was he demanding a stranger's company? Feeling that ignoring his request would do more harm than good, Maurice complied.

'What's up?' he asked indifferently. The man looked rather more intimidating up close; his nostrils were flaring ever so slightly and he had a deep sternness in his eyes that suggested he wasn't entirely pleased with Maurice.

'You didn't pay for that bag' he said.

How the hell had he seen that?

'Well, no, I didn't.'

'You're going to have to pay for it or hand it back I'm afraid' said the man.

Maurice sighed. He'd nearly gotten away with it, but it was a miniscule defeat in the grand scheme of things. He reached into his pocket to find a five pence piece; instead he found that he had no change left.

'Ah' he said. 'I haven't got the money.'

'You'll have to give me the bag then' said his foe, unmoving.

'Really?'

'Yep.'

Maurice became annoyed. He didn't want to

have to carry multiple items all the way back to his house without a carrier bag.

'It's only five p, mate' he protested.

The man approached. 'Doesn't matter' he said. 'If you can't pay for it you can't have it.'

'You couldn't just let me off this once?' asked Maurice, stepping away. 'I shop here all the time.'

'I aint seen you' he replied with a shrug. 'And if that were true you'd know that we don't give away carrier bags.'

'Listen mate' said Maurice. 'Don't bother with the sarcasm. I didn't realise you charged for them, that's all. I don't have the money this time but it isn't a big deal, is it? If it was, surely all the shops would be charging? I paid for everything inside the bag.' He reached in and took out his receipt to show it to his new adversary, who paused.

'Give it back' he eventually said, swiping for it. Maurice scowled.

'Fuck you!' he shouted angrily, throwing the receipt in the face of the man and turning to storm off. A sudden, violent grab on the shoulder stopped Maurice in his tracks.

'What did you say to me?' the man asked, furiously.

'I said-' but he did not wait for Maurice's complete reply. He snarled and threw a large fist at Maurice, which smashed him on the nose. A numb sensation followed and with no time to cry out in surprise, the man then grabbed him by both shoulders, punched him two or three more times and then thrust his knee into Maurice's gut. He bent double in pain and dropped the bag, its contents rolling out onto the pavement. But the man was no longer interested in reclaiming his prize. He violently shoved Maurice to the floor and stomped heavily on his chest to subdue him. The force was excruciating. Maurice rolled onto his side in agony and finally found time to emit that scream. Ignoring his throes, the man began kicking him in the ribs and then, as the painful response had caused Maurice to roll over, the back.

Aching from head to toe, Maurice crawled pathetically away from his attacker and managed to stand up. The man lunged at him once more, crushing the fallen sandwich in his path, and met him with multiple fists to the face and stomach. Shaken and battered, Maurice slumped back to the nearest wall and leant upon it. The rest was short lived as a sinister shadow quickly fell upon him and there was his foe once again, who took him by the arms and forced him upright.

'Don't you ever come back here again you little prick' he threatened.

Maurice's bruised, bloodshot eyes met those of his attacker. 'You cunt' he whispered defiantly. The man responded with one final blow to Maurice's chest, which caused him to collapse to the ground once more. He'd been waiting for a more severe hangover to kick in, instead he'd just been kicked in.

Barely able to register the shocked stares of the myriad high street shoppers that had amassed around him, Maurice nonetheless heard the faint sound of a siren fade into being. Justice, he thought. Someone has called the police. This terrible brute will face up to what he has done. The relief was mostly buried under his shock and terror, but at least it was there.

A car pulled up beside Maurice's crumpled body and an officer stepped out.

Maurice raised a shaking arm and pointed accusingly at his attacker, for the benefit of the officer looming above him. 'That's the guy' he groaned.

Seemingly ignoring the revelation, the officer knelt beside Maurice. He was a kind-faced man, clearly younger than he. His eyes looked deep into Maurice's and he spoke.

'Can you get up?' he asked.

With a stifled breath, Maurice nodded. He found his way to his feet with difficulty and stared indignantly past the policeman and toward the hulking frame of the man who'd beaten him and destroyed his lunch.

The officer spoke again. 'Is what I've heard correct?'

Maurice couldn't believe his ears. Surely he looked like he'd just been dropped from a skyscraper onto a bed of nails. 'Of course it is' he groaned.

'You stole a carrier bag?'

His jaw dropped, which in his state was more disconcerting than usual.

'I'm sorry?'

'The employees of this retailer told us that you left the premises having failed to pay for one of the items in your possession.'

Maurice paused. 'Yes but-'

'You are of course aware that it is a felony to take items which carry a price tag from an establishment such as this without paying?' the officer continued.

'It was a five pence carrier bag!' cried Maurice in horrified disbelief.

'The monetary value of the item in question is irrelevant.'

'That bloke just beat the absolute shit out of me!' yelled Maurice. 'Won't he be punished?'

The officer did not immediately reply. Maurice was sure he spied -though admittedly his temporarily damaged vision may have been inaccurate- a smug, victorious grin form on the face of the man who had pacified him.

'The man you have accused is employed by this retailer to ensure that shoplifters are prevented from succeeding in their crimes' said the officer, eventually.

'By beating them to death?' asked Maurice.

The officer let out a long breath. 'Given the situation described to me' he said, 'I will let you off this time. But bear in mind that if any such incident occurs again we will have no choice but to affect more serious action. Do you understand?'

Maurice wanted to scream his injustice into the face of this man until his condescending features burned up and he melted to the ground, but defiance had already cost him his optimism, his ambition and his sandwich. Instead he nodded obediently.

'Glad you understand' said the policeman, who then returned to his vehicle and swiftly departed. The victor had already returned to his throne inside the posh supermarket, no doubt swiftly back in the process of seeking out slender-bodied young shoplifters to assert his superior strength upon. Maurice stared sorrowfully at his mangled, flattened lunch and wondered how come he was the only party who'd been told off for stealing, before turning away and returning home, feeling foolish for being drawn in by the empty promise of a beautiful day.

Jo 'The Hat', who has a Boyfriend

He had a slight purple bruise around his right eye (which itself was deeply bloodshot) and his ribs ached slightly, but each of these things were fading fast and Maurice wasn't one to let something as inconsequential as a severe beating hamper his plans. He'd told Hayden all about the attack earlier that day. Hayden seemed, if at all possible, even more outraged than Maurice at the affair. While he recognised the indignation of the police taking the side of a brutal attacker over a petty thief, Maurice was mostly annoyed over losing what would probably have been the best sandwich he'd have tasted in years.

Jet Tea hadn't had his eyes away from the screen of his mobile phone for longer than two minutes at any time, discounting, of course, the time the tube spent under ground where his signal died.

He, Maurice and Hayden were on their way to a pub in London Bridge that was holding an open mic night that evening. Maurice wished to play his new song and Hayden said he might get up on stage if he was drunk enough. Jet Tea continued to think about Gemma. He'd text her earlier to invite her, despite Maurice's contentions that it was not her type of night out at all. This did not deter Jet Tea, who remained convinced that Gemma was in love with him and would sail oceans of vomit to spend time with him.

'Where is Jet Tea?' asked Maurice upon realising that only he and Hayden were now walking to the pub. Hayden shrugged, then looked behind him. The distant figure of their daydreaming friend staggered far behind, staring intently at his phone.

'Oi!' shouted Hayden, laughing. Maurice turned round to see Jet Tea and stopped in his tracks. Jet Tea looked up and his gaze widened as he realised how far behind he stood. He squealed in mild panic and picked up his pace to what might be described as a hurried skip to catch up with his friends.

'We still have to sign up you know' said Maurice.

'Sorry' replied Jet Tea. 'I thought I had a text'.

'Have you heard from her lately?' Hayden asked.

'No. She's still trying to work out how to apologise to me after that night at the Treaty.'

Maurice sighed. 'Apologise for being single and getting with a bloke she fancied?'

This annoyed Jet Tea. 'Rebounds' he grumbled. 'It's all rebounds. I shouldn't have played hard to get, I've confused her.'

Maurice laughed. 'Hard to get?' he said. 'You followed her around dancing for two nights on end then sent her about fifty text messages. You're not playing hard to get so much as hard to ignore and against those near-impossible odds she seems to be managing it. What does that tell you?' They were all, including Maurice, slightly hit by the harsh sincerity of his words. Nevertheless, they'd long since learnt that Maurice was a prolific purveyor of tough love, and he always meant well by his abruptness.

'She wants me' said a frustratingly undeterred Jet Tea, who began to stomp slightly ahead of his friends.

Through his step, Jet Tea's left leg hurtled back toward the ground but as it did so a small section of the pavement seemed to part for a second, revealing a faint purply-orange light beneath it and he stepped down further than he'd intended, causing him to trip. To his embarrassment, it seemed that the ground didn't come apart at all. Of course not. How or why would it?

Still laughing at his stumble, the three friends arrived at the pub. Maurice led the way as they entered the building.

The interior of the pub seemed too big for its capacity, which on this particular night consisted of about six middle-aged men experiencing varying degrees of baldness, a disinterested barman reading The Sun newspaper and, possibly (it may have only been a made up memory born out of iconography commonly associated with what definitely was there) a scruffy little dog drinking from a bowl by the bar. Maurice and Hayden's faces fell. Jet Tea's would have too, were it not already placed firmly downward towards his phone.

''Scuse me mate' said Maurice to the barman. The dog might have looked up from the bowl if either of those things existed.

'Downstairs' he groaned in reply, managing to notice Maurice's guitar case without having to break his gaze from the newspaper.

Of course.

The basement room of the pub couldn't have been more different from the ground floor without no longer being a pub. It was a dimly lit, narrow room with white-brick walls and a low ceiling. The bar was a slither of light on the left hand side of the room and there were lots of people, most with hair. There was almost certainly no dog. An earnest-looking young man with spectacles and a grey scarf was singing his heart out about beer on stage, accompanied by his acoustic guitar. His song finished and the disinterested applause of an audience consisting mainly of people waiting for their turn sounded him out. He bowed politely and left the stage, accidentally banging his guitar on the step.

Hayden looked over to the left side of the stage. Maurice was already over there, writing his name down on the host's clipboard. After doing so he returned to his friends.

'I put your name down just after mine' he said to Hayden in a loud whisper as the next act started.

'Ah, you prick' said Hayden angrily but quietly. 'I wasn't sure if I wanted to go on yet.'

'It's alright mate' replied Maurice. 'We're not on until near the end, plenty of time to calm your nerves with a few beers.'

'It's not nerves' hissed Hayden. 'It's

155

indifference.'

Maurice patted him on the arm. 'If it were indifference you would have no issue with playing. Calm down and get a beer.'

Hayden was halfway to the bar. 'Red wine for me' said Maurice, slightly louder than certain occupants of the room would have liked. Maurice never drank beer when he was singing, as it tended to damage his vocal cords.

Hayden returned to their corner table with two pints and a small glass of house red. Jet Tea was not around to take his pint.

'Where is he now?' asked Hayden.

Maurice simply nodded in the direction of the stage. There sat Jet Tea, by himself, staring obediently and intently at the young woman who had just arrived behind the microphone, arranging the stand to suit her height. She was dressed in a baggy green coat and a woolen, stripy coloured hat rested loosely on top of her long, brown hair. She had no instrument and looked slightly of the hippy persuasion.

'A political poet' whispered Hayden, before a sarcastic 'Wonderful.'

'At least he's not staring at his phone now' said Maurice fondly.

The woman began. Hayden was right, she was a poet. She recited her poem in a rather restless, sarcastic tone, raising her eyebrows and sighing where appropriate;

'They graffitied this town ages ago
They attacked all the walls, all the houses and side
roads.
They desecrated beauty and perfect design
With dull grey brick, coke adverts and ugly signs

See I'm not speaking of yobs with paint cans
Who tiptoe at night to share with the land
Their messages and beliefs, their integrity
I speak of the industries that attack you and me

Did we ask for a message of freedom and love
To be painted in colour below and above?
No we didn't but did we ask companies
To paint power and greed up and down our streets?

I don't think we did, so why is it I
That will be attacked when I'm caught in their sights?
Why not attack the billboards with their outstretched
hands

Demanding the money from all over the land?

'Cause they tarnished our streets long before I came
With my paint can and message, not selling my name
It is they that graffiti, and they do in plain sight
While my message of love must be shadowed by the
night.'

She smiled as she finished reciting. The room erupted in applause. Maurice and Hayden applauded politely.

'What did you think?' whispered Hayden.

'A bit trite' said Maurice. 'Heard all that before.'

'That's the thing about open mic nights I suppose.'

'Yep.'

Jet Tea was applauding with severe enthusiasm and continued to do so as she left the stage. When she headed over to the bar he jumped out of his chair and approached her.

He frantically brainstormed the best things to start a conversation with. Her colourful hat stood out.

'Your hat looks like a sock' Jet Tea blurted

before introducing himself. 'Where did you get it?'

The woman spun round with a start. She smiled politely. 'I'm sorry?'

'I want a hat like yours, it looks like a sock.'

'It is a sock' she said. 'My dad has gigantism of the left foot and this is one of his socks.'

Jet Tea found that fascinating. 'Really?' he asked.

The hat-sock girl sighed like she did when she recited her poem. 'I'm just joking' she said. 'I made it.' Jet Tea nodded with embarrassment.

'That was a great poem' he said. 'Was it about graffiti?'

She raised an eyebrow, trying to decide if her lyrics were more implicit than she'd realised or if this man talking to her was a big idiot.

'Yes, it was' she said. 'My name is Jo, I'm a street artist.'

Jet Tea shook Jo's hand. 'A street artist?'

'Yeah. I paint pictures in the streets, rather than cheap, incoherent graffiti tags.'

'Okay.'

'Have you ever seen that picture of the Elephant being mugged on Charing Cross Road?'

Jet Tea hadn't. 'Yes' he replied. 'I like that

one.'

'Yeah, I painted that' Jo replied, proudly.

'My name is Jet Tea' said Jet Tea.

'Jet Tea?' Jo replied. 'That's an odd name. Do you have Asian relatives?'

Jet Tea had no idea how or why that had crossed her mind. 'No' he said. 'It's a nickname my friend Maurice gave to me. He's playing later, he's amazing.'

'What does it mean?'

'What does what mean?'

'Your nickname' said Jo. 'What does it mean?'

'Oh right, I think it's because I love tea so much. I don't know, you'll have to ask Maurice.'

'Okay' said Jo. 'And what about the "Jet" part?'

'It's my initials' Jet Tea replied, wondering why she wouldn't have assumed that.

'Fair enough. What does "JET" stand for?'

'J-' Jet Tea began, but paused as the room fell silent and the next act took to the stage.

A lot of earnest-sounding acoustic artists filled the ensuing night, as well as at least two other poets. Jet Tea wasn't really listening to them. He hadn't rejoined his friends (except once to collect the beer Hayden had

160

bought for him), but instead managed to keep talking to Jo. He danced out mocking gestures to any act that he thought deserved it, and Jo giggled occasionally. They spoke of street art; Jet Tea continued to mildly insult Jo by accidentally referring to it as 'graffiti', and they spoke about food once Jet Tea had mentioned his job, and how stressful it was becoming. He mentioned Gemma only once, and didn't mention Tara at all.

They stopped talking when Maurice eventually took to the stage, and they enjoyed his time up there, even the Dolly Parton cover. However, each of them struggled to maintain interest in Hayden's performance, which was an improvised ballad, entitled *Months of the Year* and consisted of a slurred ten-line verse for each month from January through to December, complete with pauses to allow for beer-swigs. At one point Jet Tea had glanced around to the sound man who was frantically waving his arms in a 'stop, please' gesture. Thankfully, the song only lasted until July because that was around the time Hayden had run out of beer and lost interest in playing.

Hayden was the last act, and he'd managed to do a good deal of the bouncer's job by clearing most of the room. Before long only he, Maurice, Jet Tea and Jo remained.

'So I think I'm gonna head back' said Jo with the same polite smile she'd first greeted him with. Jet Tea turned frantic.

'Really?' he asked.

'Yeah' Jo continued. Her next words sounded, to Jet Tea, dreadfully slow and echoed ominously as each one of them deftly punched a different part of his circulatory system; '*My boyfriend will be home soon and he doesn't have a key*'.

Jet Tea issued a slow head swivel and intense glare at Maurice, who returned a sympathetic, knowing nod.

'Well we're going to a club' said Jet Tea. 'Where do you live?'

'Dalston' replied Jo.

'The club is in Dalston!' said Jet Tea hopefully. 'Why don't you come after you've let him in?'

Jo shrugged and tilted her head as she pondered the possibility. 'Yeah, maybe' she said. I'll give you my number and you can text me details. Jet Tea was slightly concerned that she didn't ask for his number, because (though he'd never admit it), not having his number implied that she wouldn't be overly bothered were he never to contact her.

He took Jo's number and saved it in his

phonebook as 'Jo 'The Hat' Who Has a Boyfriend', because Jet Tea liked to add descriptions to people's names when he took their numbers (Hayden, for instance, was saved as 'Hayden Crazy 1 with the 2 Beers'). This was quite possibly an act of defiance against his dyslexia.

They parted ways. Jet Tea could not shake the image of never seeing Jo 'The Hat' again. It was actually two images; one was simply a black square, while the other was Jet Tea himself, in third person, staring expressionlessly at a blank wall.

As they walked to the tube station Jet Tea began desperately looking up night clubs in Dalston on Hayden's phone. Armed with a list of search results, he then started attempting to whittle the list down to one of venues suitable for a cool graffiti artist-poet girl with a stripy, self-made hat. Eventually, with Maurice's supervision, he settled for a place. Seven pounds to get in and six minutes' walk from the nearest tube station, promising an 'eclectic' mix of indie rock, ska punk and metal.

He sent Jo a text with the name and location of the club, followed by a short request '*Make me a sock hat pls.*'

Jet Tea sat on the tube and didn't lean back once. He spent the entire (admittedly short) journey grinning and patting his knees like a reputable drummer. Maurice and Hayden spoke about their night at the open mic. Hayden was hungry and Maurice was expressing concern about leaving his guitar in the pub. Hayden reassured him that bar staff are very much faithful when it comes to looking after a customer's belongings.

They arrived at the club after roughly an eight-and-a-half minute walk. It was a detached building on a corner. A burger van stood outside.

'Ah,' said Hayden wishfully as he noticed the van. 'I want food.'

'Let's get a burger' said Maurice.

Jet Tea, though fairly hungry, wanted nothing more than to get straight into the club and find Jo. He didn't care that logically she could not possibly be there before them as they'd left first and she had to go home to let her boyfriend in. Christ, he didn't even care that she had a boyfriend. Maybe that was Tara's fault; she had a boyfriend for a substantial portion of their relationship, the *better* portion of their relationship, in fact.

'You getting a burger?' Hayden asked Jet Tea.

'Dunno' Jet Tea replied, staring at the doors of the night club like a dog on a lead staring at its master's front door. 'Do they have chicken?'

Hayden had forgotten that Jet Tea didn't like beef. He glanced from the menu behind the counter to the visible grill, noticing no chicken on either. 'I don't think so' he said.

Jet Tea sighed. 'No thanks then.'

He waited patiently (but not necessarily comfortably) as his friends ate their burgers. Maurice looked at his agitated friend with sympathy. 'Want a bite?' he asked.

Jet Tea couldn't ignore his hunger. Yes, it was beef, but he should probably eat *something* if he was about to get severely drunk. 'Go on then' he concluded.

Maurice passed his half-finished beef burger to Jet Tea. Jet Tea took a big bite, mentally noting that the meat was too thin to be grilled for as long as it was and that the bread should have been covered if they weren't going to toast it.

As he chewed, he received a tap on the shoulder from behind. He spun round with excitement.

It wasn't Jo 'The Hat'. It was a man in a white shirt with greasy hair and a big camera. For some reason he took a photo of Jet Tea eating, gave him a thumbs up and walked off. Jet Tea, slightly confused but ultimately indifferent, passed the burger back to Maurice and shrugged the incident off.

The process of entering a nightclub tends to be absurdly familiar, regardless on whether one has ever even set foot into that particular nightclub. For Jet Tea and friends, the nightclub in Dalston, which none of them had ever been to, was no exception. They queued for around five minutes, were met with a brief but accusatory stare from the bouncer in charge of the door before being approved for entry with a consenting wave, anxiously and excitedly descended a narrow flight of stairs and arrived at a booth at the bottom. There, they each gave a ten-pound note to a friendly looking woman who dressed and acted like this was the last club she'd willingly be seen in on a night off, and each received three pounds in change. Hayden received a two-pound coin in his change, the others didn't.

That wasn't important. What was important to Jet Tea as he entered the main room of the club and the faint, muffled bass gave way to loud, bouncy indie music as the double doors opened, was whether or not Jo was here.

Maurice and Hayden danced to the tired strains

of *Smells Like Teen Spirit*, *Common People* and *One Step Beyond* while Jet Tea stared at the door longingly. He sipped weak beer from a plastic bottle and eventually decided to join his friends in a dance.

Stretching his arms out elaborately to ensure Maurice and Hayden distanced themselves, Jet Tea proceeded to dance with incredible energy, flicking his long hair and staring dreamily toward the ceiling as he jittered from side to side. His arms fell straight by his sides and his hands pointed outwards in a somewhat feminine manner as he danced. At this point, Jo walked in.

Without seeing her, Jet Tea noticed her. Then he looked down from the ceiling. Jo was lit up by blue and green lights and a big screen on the far wall showing a slideshow of people at the night club having a good time. She hadn't put her long, green coat in the cloakroom, which Jet Tea decided made her cool. Maurice and Hayden seemed to have disappeared. Jo looked around her in slight confusion for a moment, then spotted Jet Tea. She approached.

She hadn't brought her boyfriend!

'You were quick' said Jet Tea, pretending he hadn't just waited seventy-four years for her to arrive.

'I didn't go home in the end' said Jo 'The Hat'.

'My friends are round, so they let my boyfriend in.'

Jet Tea hadn't stopped dancing, by the way.

'Your friends were round?' asked Jet Tea. 'How come you didn't know?'

Jo giggled. 'We're a pretty tight group' she shouted over the music. 'They all have keys to my place.'

'Really?' asked Jet Tea in a forced falsetto. 'That's a bit strange.'

'Strange?' asked Jo. 'Says you who dances like that and sends a girl you've just met a text asking her to make you a hat.'

'Did you make me a hat?' shouted Jet Tea.

'Not yet' laughed Jo.

'Last woman I'll trust!'

Jo patted Jet Tea on the shoulder, slightly interrupting his moves. 'I have to get the materials first.'

Jo and Jet Tea changed colour as the photo slideshow progressed and the lights changed.

'Where do you get the materials from?' asked Jet Tea.

'The vegan market in Stoke Newington' Jo replied.

Jet Tea thought of his mum. 'Are you a vegan?' he cried, trying to outdo the thumping bass.

'I'm a vegetarian' shouted Jo in reply.

If you ask Jet Tea today (you'd have to find him first), he'll probably tell you that he still doesn't know why he said the following;

'Awesome!' he replied. 'I'm also a vegetarian.' Then he leant in to hug Jo.

They hugged in celebration of vegetarianism, and Jo smiled sweetly. Then she glanced over at the big screen on the far wall. The image changed from that of four girls laughing and waving glowsticks, to a rather familiar face.

There, seven feet high and glowing intently back at Jo, was Jet Tea's big face, wide-eyed and enthusiastic, holding a half-eaten beef burger and chewing. Thick, mangled chunks of grey-brown beef, marinated in saliva and thick grease, had set up camp around his lips and chin. Jo's hands fell slowly from Jet Tea's sides. Jet Tea, wondering why Jo 'The Hat' had broken off the hug, decided to look in the direction she was looking in.

He stood as still and silent as she did. *That's* why the man outside was taking photos.

The image hung in the darkness for several seconds. Neither Jet Tea nor Jo could move. From somewhere in the crowd, two familiar voices cheered.

Eventually the nightmare image was replaced by a photo of a topless fat man, pulling a triumphant face and raising a fist in the air. Jo flashed Jet Tea a judgemental stare, which seemed to last until his next birthday. Then she broke it and laughed.

'Well timed, that' she yelled.

Jet Tea went red, and this was noticeable even under the bright yellow light on his face.

'Drink?' he asked.

He had survived what he will forevermore refer to as 'the incident with the burger'. He'd bought Jo a drink and the two of them danced to over-rated, over-played indie rock. Jo periodically took her mobile phone out and looked at it.

'This club is quite shit' she said, eventually.

Jet Tea pictured her leaving him forever and panicked. Hayden and Maurice had already gone home, if Jo now left he'd have to call it a night, and he didn't want to.

'What do you want to do now?' Jet Tea asked in desperation.

'There's still a few people at mine' said Jo. 'Think they're having a few drinks if you want to come over.'

170

Jet Tea's face lit up, because of the disco lights, really. 'Won't your boyfriend find that a bit weird?' he asked.

Jo waved her hand dismissively. 'He went to bed ages ago' she said. 'Anyway, most of my friends are guys.'

'Yeah alright' said Jet Tea, trying his hand at an insincerely casual response.

Then he experienced one of the most exciting night-bus journeys he'd had in months.

Jessica the Vegan

There was a sleeping fat man who fell forward with the jolt of the moving bus and landed face-first into the lap of the disgusted young woman opposite him. There was a rodent-like hooded man with a face clouded by matted brown hair, whispering foreboding incoherencies into his jittery hands. There was an old lady nodding gently with the movement of the bus. Finally, there was Jet Tea, a mop-headed little man in a Pixies t-shirt sitting at the back of the bus next to an attractive, hippy-looking woman with a colourful hat. He clenched his hands periodically and tried admirably not to wear his excitement on his body. They were headed to her house, after all.

Jet Tea and Jo chatted away amidst the gallery

of oddballs that regularly ride night buses. Evening-workers and the young and drunk aside, a night bus is the eternal haunt of the emotionally lost and mentally free. The concerned woman whose lap was recently met by an inflated, snoring head meekly pushed said head away from her knees, causing its owner to snort in alarm and wake up, briefly. The jittery rodent man growled a sentence that ended with the words 'hero's death'.

Luckily for Jet Tea, he was able to properly translate Jo's guarded dialogue into its correct meaning. He congratulated himself at possessing this ability as he processed her words.

'I hope you don't find it weird that I invited you to my house after only just meeting you' became '*You instantly took my breath away and as such I refuse to endure the traditional rigmarole of getting to know a guy before initiating relations when the guy is as amazing as you*'.

'No worries' replied Jet Tea, tactful to both translations. 'What's done is done.'

'I'm a very outgoing person and I have a lot of male friends, so don't read into it too much' became '*Whatever I may say to discourage you, just know that I really want you. My excuses are only there to maintain my dignity. Once we have entered the privacy of my*

174

home I am completely at your mercy.'

Jet Tea didn't realise he had the vocabulary to make such translations. Impressed and surprised, he laughed out loud. Jo seemed shocked.

'Erm, you remember I have a boyfriend, right?' became '*Yes, there is currently another man in my life but such as the seasons change, your recent arrival into my world has instantly rendered him obsolete and he will shortly be old news.'*

Jet Tea rubbed his hands together (when Jo wasn't looking) with glee as the bus turned its final corner and the cold, automated female voice read out their final destination.

Jo's flat was dimly lit and had no seating in the living room. Despite all this, and despite the small cluster of accusatory looks beaming from the faces of her friends and housemates, the place seemed rather comfortable.

'Sorry we have no chairs' said Jo. 'You don't mind sitting on the floor, do you?'

'It's alright, I'm usually treated worse,' Jet Tea replied, trying to make self-deprecation sound charming. Jo smiled sweetly. A success.

Jet Tea shifted awkwardly among the people on

the floor until he found space enough to seat himself. He sat down next to a young lady in a grey jumper, sporting a modest brown ponytail and a sullen facial expression. Jet Tea caught her eye and it shortly became difficult for him to look away. There was something in her undressed facial features that urged him to try and learn all about her. Jo had wandered into the kitchen and he had nobody else to talk to, not knowing who anyone was.

'What's your name?' he asked.

'Jessica' she replied. Her pseudo-frown remained unchanged.

'I'm Jet Tea.'

'What do you do?' asked Jessica, in a somewhat condescending tone.

'I'm a chef in a pub' Jet Tea replied.

'Oh right, does that mean you chop up animals and that?' she asked, her words doing little to replace a sarcastic snigger.

Jet Tea felt slightly embarrassed. 'Well, yeah' he replied, 'depends on the dish.'

'So I take it you eat meat?'

'So I take it you're a vegetarian?'

Jessica seemed pleased. 'Vegan, as it goes' she said. 'Me and my boyfriend are both vegans.' She gestured over to a man crouched in the closest corner, writing something in a small notebook. He did not look up. Despite her slight hostility, Jet Tea was rather stung upon hearing the word 'boyfriend'. He couldn't figure out what it was, and he probably wasn't even aware that it existed, but something about Jessica was extremely attractive.

'My mum's a vegan' said Jet Tea.

'Good for her. What about you?'

'No' said Jet Tea, mentally shaking off the incident with the burger, 'but I respect vegetarians.'

Jessica huffed at this remark. To her that was about as comforting to her way of life as an afternoon in an abattoir, implying that meat is an overwhelmingly addictive drug that successfully giving up would be a miracle in human will-power. Jet Tea made vegetarianism sound as admirable and intimidating as fire-fighting or volunteering to work night shifts in a lunatic asylum.

'Why do you eat meat?' She asked.

'Because I like it' Jet Tea replied. 'Simple as.'

Simple as. No, it wasn't simple at all.

'Even though it's really, really bad for you?'

This annoyed Jet Tea, who was now finally ready to give the argument his all. 'I drink beer as well' he said. 'That's bad for us, but we still do it.'

'Well I don't drink either' replied Jessica.

Jet Tea opened his mouth, then closed it again. 'Good for you.'

'Did you know some red meat remains clogged in your digestive system for years on end?' asked Jessica. 'It's pretty much indigestible to humans.'

'Actually I don't eat red meat.'

'And cows can sense death for weeks upon weeks as they're waiting to be slaughtered' Jessica continued, ignoring Jet Tea's last remark.

'When it's cheap meat, yeah' said Jet Tea.

'What?'

'Cheaply sourced beef is bad news, I agree' he continued. 'But I buy free range meat when I'm cooking, and I make sure any kitchen I work in does as well.'

'But' Jessica paused. 'The cow still dies.'

'Yeah but cows don't actually have a human sense of death-'

'-sentient' Jessica's boyfriend chimed in, without looking up from his notebook.

'What? They don't have that conscious fear of dying, so from the cow's point of view, it has a nice life running around fields and that, then it's gone. The method of killing is humane and quick so the cow is dead before it even realises something is going on.'

'Humane' scoffed Jessica. 'You don't use the words "humane" and "ethical" when people are being murdered, do you?'

'That's not the same.'

'How isn't it?'

'Because we have rights' said Jet Tea, wishing he'd prepared a better comeback than that. He predicted the counter-argument down to the word.

'What about animal rights?'

'What, the rights animals aren't sentryent enough to come up with-'

'-Sentient' the boyfriend said again.

'-so humans impose them instead?'

Jessica scowled. 'That's not how animal rights work.'

Jet Tea found he was agreeing with Jessica more than he was letting on. He was largely playing devil's advocate at this point in the conversation.

'How can they be animal rights if they're imposed by humans? How do we know we haven't misinterpretated the animals and they actually want to die?'

'Misinterpreted' said Jessica's boyfriend, still

writing.

'Sorry?' said Jet Tea.

'It's misinterpreted' said Jessica. 'You said misinterpret-ated. You basically made up a word.'

Jet Tea was embarrassed. 'All words are made up words' he said defiantly. 'Mine just haven't caught on yet.'

'Whatever' said Jessica. 'The will to survive is clearly evident in all the species we kill for food. We haven't "misinterpretated" anything, you idiot.'

'Anyway, I believe in animal rights' said Jet Tea, ignoring the slur and deciding to approach the argument from a different perspective. 'That's why I eat panda.'

Jessica made a poor attempt at hiding her astonishment. 'What?' she asked.

'Pandas want to die' he continued. 'They refuse to mate, that's a basic animal urge that they're fighting. They clearly want their species to die out, so who am I to deny them that right? Eating panda is basically euthanasia. You're for euthanasia, aren't you? People like you usually are.'

Jessica didn't believe Jet Tea's obvious lie, but the desired effect of winding her up beyond belief was working. 'People like me?' she repeated angrily.

'You know, vegans, graffiti, going to protests and all that' said Jet Tea.

'It's not graffiti it's street art' said Jo, who, for some reason, Jet Tea hadn't noticed was back in the room. 'It's good graffiti, nicer to look at than a grey brick wall.'

Jet Tea looked round. 'We were just talking about meat' he said.

'I know, I heard you pissing off my friends' Jo replied testily.

'How am I pissing anyone off? It's just a debate!'

Jessica smiled. 'Jet Tea eats meat' she said.

'I know' said Jo, mentally shaking off the incident with the burger.

'To be fair' said Jet Tea, 'I would be a vegetarian, I just love chicken. And you don't really get the chance to be away from meat in my job.'

Jessica's boyfriend glanced up from his notebook. 'Fucking carnivore, think for yourself' said the man who used to eat KFC and call women 'slags' until he met a vegan that he wanted to have sex with. Jet Tea ignored him. He could have said that nobody ever urged him to eat meat, and he was even brought up in a vegetarian home, so how exactly was his decision to eat meat any more an example of being blindly led than that of someone who changes their diet based on what their friends are doing? He left this argument to himself and remained silent.

'My point is,' Jessica continued, 'that I don't agree with eating meat. I'm not comfortable with the way the animal is treated and I don't like the fact that so many people don't seem to have a problem with it. Society is broken because too many people are indifferent to things that they should be horrified by.' Jet Tea noticed that, with every syllable uttered by Jessica, her head gently nodded and shook as though she was agreeing with and congratulating herself with every point she made.

'What about Kobe beef?' asked Jet Tea.

'What's that?' Jessica asked.

'It's like the poshest beef you can get.' Jet Tea replied. 'Japanese or something. It goes by the idea that, the better the animal is treated, the better the meat. The cow is given a huge section of land to roam on, fed regularly with fresh grain and beer, it's treated better than most humans. It's basically treated like a king.'

'Yeah but kings aren't murdered at the end of their reign' said Jessica, very much emphasising the word 'murdered.'

'I think your history teacher needs a disciplinary' said Jet Tea. Jessica's boyfriend let out a small giggle and promptly clapped a hand over his mouth in embarrassment. 'Kobe beef doesn't exist' he eventually mumbled.

'Listen' said Jet Tea. 'I eat meat, you don't. You have your reasons, why do you have to turn food into a lifestyle? Just be happy that you clearly have a healthier diet than me and are less likely to die from heart failure.'

Jessica tutted. 'You idiot. You don't know what you're talking about' she hissed.

'What? I've cooked more meals than you've had hot dinners!' said Jet Tea, trying not to think too hard about what he'd just said. He turned to Jo, 'I like your friend' he said. 'She's passionate.'

'What do you think of Jet Tea?' Jo asked Jessica, trying to suppress a laugh.

'I think he's probably a wanker, though I'm still getting to know him' Jessica replied.

Jet Tea smiled. 'That's about right' he said. 'Sorry if I offended you, but I was trying to.'

'I thought as much' said Jessica. 'But I still think you're a bloody caveman.' It's funny how people use the term 'caveman' as a way of insulting intelligence. After all, it was the caveman who had the idea of evolving into an intelligent, dominant species. That was rather clever, although Jessica and her boyfriend would likely disagree.

Jet Tea was enjoying the evening's discussion, and he soon worked out that Jessica's challenging defiance was what made her so attractive. He sat all evening with his back to her boyfriend as they argued relentlessly.

'Did you know a cow can go upstairs but not down?' asked Jet Tea, attempting to project a level of intelligence that could match that of his adversary.

'That's probably because the only staircases cows tend to climb are in slaughterhouses' she replied. Jet Tea laughed.

Eventually the two of them had run out of things to argue about and, subconsciously realising that, despite everything, they didn't hate each other, began to head towards a more pleasant conversation.

'I'm in love with your friend Jo' said Jet Tea, the first time he'd admitted it to anyone, not least himself. But was he silently disagreeing with himself as he said it? He couldn't be sure.

'I thought as much' said Jessica, 'why else would you willingly spend an entire evening in a room full of vegetarians?'

'Reckon she likes me?'

'I couldn't say. She has a boyfriend, you know.'

Jet Tea glanced over his shoulder at Jessica's boyfriend, who had said next to nothing all evening. 'He seems happy' he joked.

'Fuck off, prick' said the boyfriend.

'And he knows my name!' cried Jet Tea, forcing Jessica to fight a smile. Her boyfriend looked up.

'Did you have lessons in how to be a prick?' he asked. 'Or did you learn by ear?'

'Easy, Craig' said Jessica. Craig mumbled bitterly and returned to his notebook.

'What is he writing?' asked Jet Tea.

'He likes to take notes when he meets someone new' said Jessica. 'They're really interesting.'

Jet Tea was slightly confused as to the purpose of this. 'So he's biographising me?' he asked, unintentionally making up another word.

'Why don't you get annoyed?' asked Jessica. 'We've been pretty much insulting you all night, most men would have become pissed off by now.'

Jet Tea shrugged. He couldn't think of an answer to that, as he'd never really thought about it.

From his perspective he was annoyed all the time.

When the night had become morning, as such reaching an end and Jet Tea was strolling home, he sent a text message to Hayden;

Im in love with a girl with a boyfriend it read.

I already know was Hayden's immediate reply, having witnessed Jet Tea's behaviour at the open mic and in the club first-hand. But Jet Tea quickly realised that Hayden didn't actually know, because he also realised that he didn't mean Jo 'The Hat'. Jet Tea was now head over heels in love with Jessica, the vegan who called him an idiot, a wanker and a caveman all in one night. He also thought of an answer to her question. He sent another text, this time to Jo 'The Hat';

Tell ur friend Jessac I dont get angry because a little man like me wood get beaten up if I did.

Jet Tea Fucks Up

Weekdays away from work are very special to people who don't have nine-to-five, Monday-to-Friday jobs. The pubs aren't too busy, a seat on the tube is easily attainable and, if you are Jet Tea (in which case, hello Jet Tea. Hope you're enjoying your biography), mum's at work and the house is free. Occasionally, his ever changing work roster would coincidentally give him a Friday evening off, followed by Saturday and Sunday free before a return on Monday morning, like all those regular people who he'd never met. On these occasions he was continually underwhelmed by this vastly over-rated, internationally-worshipped concept. Two consecutive days, during which every pub, restaurant, park and motorway are too overcrowded to really enjoy, then an early start which limits what one can really get up to on the latter of those days off. Weekends aren't all that, although obviously a nine-to-fiver would never learn this. Thus the weekend worship never wanes.

This particular weekday, which was a Tuesday that may or may not go down in local history as *That* Tuesday (it is too early to tell) began with some of that cheery optimism Jet Tea had picked up on the toilet seat of the Treaty the day Tara dumped him. He made his compulsory day-off fry up and blasted the Pixies' *There Goes My Gun* at tinnitus-inducing volume throughout the house as he roamed the grounds in only a pair of boxers and his new favourite t-shirt, his thoughts flinging constantly from Jo 'The Hat' to her friend Jessica. Jo 'The Hat' had a boyfriend, which gave Jessica the edge. Jessica also had a boyfriend, but he was obviously a wanker and no match for Jet Tea.

As mid-afternoon approached and the weather promised to be a good boy, Jet Tea began entertaining the idea of having a couple of beers. The day was his, and its future was riddled with endless possible outcomes. No despicable, unwritten societal rule would stop him from having a beer earlier than people think he should, today.

After a few sips Jet Tea wiped the condensation

from his hands onto his Pixies t-shirt and gave Hayden a call.

''Ello mate' said Jet Tea.

'Alright' replied Hayden.

'Do you fancy coming round for a few beers?'

'Now?'

'Yeah.'

'Erm,' Hayden hesitated. He more or less always agreed to plans such as these, but was never comfortable just giving his decision there and then.

'I don't really have much money.'

'It's alright I've already got beers.'

'Yeah but for the bus, I mean.'

Jet Tea looked wistfully at the beautiful day outside, ignoring the dark clouds that loomed distantly in the corners of his periphery. Then he glanced at his beer bottle from which he'd only had a couple of sips. Not over the limit by any means.

'I'll give you a lift, if you want.'

'Really?'

'Yeah, I don't mind.'

Now Hayden had free booze, a free lift and a free afternoon. There really was little reason to refuse this offer.

'Yeah go on then' he said. Then 'fuck it',

which in this context actually meant 'let's do it'.

After hanging up, Jet Tea then phoned Maurice.

'Woooaaeeeeyy!' shouted Maurice when he answered.

Jet Tea giggled. 'Alright?'

'Yeah mate!'

'Do you want to come over?'

'What the fuck for?' Maurice seemed a little excited already, for some reason.

'Just a few beers with me and Hayden' said Jet Tea.

'Bit early innit?'

'It's nearly one.'

'Yeeeeaaaaaaaahhh! I've already had a couple.'

'Have you? What's the occasion?'

'It's a nice day, eh!'

'Fair enough. That's what I thought.'

'Woooo! You useless fucking pisshead!'

'How is it too early if you're already drunk?'

Maurice burst into laughter and the line cut out.

Half an hour later, Hayden was in the passenger seat of Jet Tea's car on the way back to his house. They pulled up to a red traffic light and something that one of those people who cares about cars would likely refer to as 'a well nice car' pulled up next to them. A slightly doughy but broad-shouldered young man with a white shirt and too much hair gel sat in the driver's seat. A young woman with a genuinely affectionate countenance in a grey cardigan sat next to him.

Hayden glanced at the car with mild curiosity and read the number plate;

ROB 1W.

'Alright, Rob!' Hayden shouted over to the man, in jest. Jet Tea looked around; so did the man, who said nothing at first.

'Who's that?' Jet Tea asked Hayden.

'It's Rob' he replied, giggling like a child. 'Look at the number plate.'

Jet Tea's confused frown slowly inverted into a delighted grin as he beheld the plate in question. 'Hi, Rob!' he shouted.

Rob winced with poison in his eyes. He didn't notice that the woman next to him was laughing quietly. 'Fuck you' he said. Then, looking accusingly at Jet Tea's car, top to bottom, before gesturing to his own, 'you'll never be able to afford a car like this. Fucking gays.'

191

Jet Tea and Hayden paused, then burst into laughter. The light turned green.

'Bye Rob!' they each shouted as Rob revved his engine and sped off ahead of them, as though he was running away.

'What a dick' mumbled Hayden as they continued their journey.

When they pulled up, they saw Maurice standing at the front door, in a calling stance with his arms outstretched from his sides, shouting.

'JET TEA! YOU CUNT! OPEN THE FUCKING DOOR! WOOOAAYY!'

Jet Tea honked the car horn and Maurice spun around to see the car. The driver emerged from it and a newly delighted Maurice leapt upon him with a mighty hug.

The three friends sat in the kitchen shouting to each other over the animalistic screams of Black Francis on the Pixies song *Tame*. Hayden clutched an acoustic guitar on which he strummed the occasional, idle chord. Maurice was drumming along to the song on his shins and Jet Tea kept glancing hopefully at his phone.

'Heard from Gemma lately?' Hayden asked.

'Huh?' he replied. 'Jo…'

Hayden raised an eyebrow. 'Are you texting Gemma again, or that girl you were with the other night?'

Jet Tea remained transfixed on his phone screen. 'Jessica?'

'Was that her name?' asked Hayden. 'She had a stripy hat that you thought looked like a sock.'

'Oh. Jo 'The Hat'' said Jet Tea. 'She wants me.'

Hayden grimaced. 'She has a boyfriend. Who's Jessica?'

'The girl I text you about.'

'So she's the girl with the boyfriend?'

'Yeah. She wants me as well.'

'Yet she *has a boyfriend.*'

Maurice leant in. 'It's remarkable how many girls seem to prefer you to the boyfriends that they're mysteriously refusing to break up with' he yelled above the music.

Jet Tea didn't listen.

'So who are you interested in?' asked a frustrated Hayden.

'Hmm? They both want me.'

Jet Tea's new catchphrase was beginning to

irritate his friends. Hayden shrugged, got out of his seat and paused the music.

'Listen to this' he said and began playing a song on the guitar. A jolly-sounding folk song with absolutely venomous lyrics;

'Rob Rage, act your age
Not your dick size
I could never afford a car like yours
But I look on the bright side
Your shirt, your hair gel too
Well they look lovely
I was only being nice to you
So why don't you love me?

Spit on me then drive away
But your girlfriend finds us funny,
Like your number plate
You can't make me angry
If you call me gay
But you'll always be angry
Rob Rage

In West London you're never safe
So you stay wary

Anybody who speaks to you
You find a little scary
We were just trying to have some fun
No need to take it the wrong way
Hope your riches make you happy
Hope your girlfriend dies, one day

Your daddy pays for you
You're friends with your car
A little smile from me
Would do more good than harm.'

Then he repeated the chorus, via an earnest key change that made for a joyous and triumphant denouement to the song. Maurice laughed heartily, and Jet Tea giggled.

'What the hell is that about?' Maurice shouted through the laughter.

'Didn't we tell you?' replied Hayden.

'Nah.'

Jet Tea and Hayden briefly relayed the tale of 'Rob Rage' to Maurice, inevitably appointing themselves the protagonists of said tale.

'And his fucking girlfriend was sitting there laughing at him' said Jet Tea.

'Yeah,' said Hayden. 'But did you notice her face when he looked back at her?'

'No…'

'She was right obedient' he continued. 'She was straining at him lovingly while he… fucking… snotted his manly dominance all over his shit car.'

Hayden was getting drunker. His syntax sat on the precipice of senselessness and his friends braced themselves for the inevitable onslaught of fervent, baseless criticism and accusation.

'Cos he's a fucking wife-beater rapist' he slurred. Jet Tea winced.

'Whoa,' yelled Maurice. 'Where did you draw that conclusion? Do you know the guy?'

'You think everyone's a rapist' Jet Tea added.

'No' growled Hayden before a considerable swig from his beer bottle. 'I just know who *is* a rapist. I know people. Rob Rage was a right fucking manly-man wanker greasy office boy rapist.'

'Am I a rapist?' asked Maurice, humoring him.

'No.'

'Am I?' laughed Jet Tea.

'No. You aint… fucking… footballers' he slurred.

Maurice cocked his head with confusion.

196

'What? You can't make jokes about rape, Hayden. It's not on.'

'I'm not joking' Hayden shouted. 'All footballers are rapists.'

'What makes you think that?' asked Jet Tea.

'Cos… they're all rapists. It's obvious. They're a big gang of sweaty, muscle-bound millionaires. They get what they want, and they're all rapists.'

Maurice bit his tongue. 'I reckon you're talking out of your arse.'

'Fuck you' replied Hayden. 'I know it's true.'

'Can you prove it?' asked Jet Tea.

'I don't need to. I'm comfortable in my belief that all footballers are rapists.'

'*Gary Linekar?*' cried Maurice.

'Yeah him too' said Hayden. 'Listen, I'm completely certain that all footballers are rapists. There will never be any credible evidence that suggests otherwise. You can't disprove a negative. You can't prove that ghosts don't exist, you can't prove that football players aren't rapists.'

'So' Maurice began. 'What if decades pass and not a single woman ever admits to being raped by a footballer?'

'That doesn't prove me wrong.'

'Yes it does!'

'No it fucking doesn't. All the victims may have taken a vow of silence for whatever reason. All that proves is that victims of footballer rape aren't willing to talk about it.'

Jet Tea buried his head in his hands. He'd had enough of this conversation. He got out of his chair and put the Pixies album back on. Unfortunately the deafening sounds of their angry guitars did little to drown out Maurice and Hayden's pointless debate. All he wanted to do was talk about Jo 'The Hat', and Jessica. No. All he wanted to do was be with them. Talking about them would have been an adequate second-best.

'They could do a DNA test' Hayden yelled, 'they could do a DNA test and all that would prove is that one particular woman hasn't been raped by a footballer yet. They are disgusting human beings. Anyone who could feel good about earning seventy grand a week for spending an hour and a half running round a field and threatening referees *must* be a rapist.'

'The DNA test is pointless' said Maurice. 'That would only prove that the footballer had sex with the woman in question. It could have been consensual.'

'Or she could be lying out of fear' said Hayden. 'Maurice, there is *nothing* you can ever say to convince me that footballers aren't rapists. That is my belief, and it satisfies me.'

'Well fuck you' Maurice shouted in reply. 'I believe they're not.'

'That isn't a belief' said Hayden. 'That's the absence of belief.'

'No, you're wrong. That is the belief in the non-existence of something. I live by it and therefore it is still a belief.' Maurice finished his beer, slammed the bottle on to the kitchen floor, and continued. 'I'm secure in my beliefs and the way I live my life and your pointless, non-disprovable rhetoric won't detract from that.'

'I'm right' mumbled Hayden.

Somehow, against all better judgment (well, not so much against it as in the absence of it), the three of them ended up on a train toward central London. The day had passed beyond moving on and going home and now the only reasonable conclusion was to amplify the daytime drunkenness with an evening session in the lively Capital. Maurice, who was already rather tipsy when Jet Tea phoned him earlier that afternoon, was still locked in an intoxicated, heated discussion with Hayden, who had managed to make short work of expelling his sobriety thanks in large part to his unrelenting weakness for alcohol; they'd purchased a few cans of lager for the train journey. Fortunately, the discussion had moved on from rape. Unfortunately, it had become about a particular, barely legal Reality TV star that had, of recent weeks, continually made the front page (thanks to her predisposition of showering in a tight bikini a short distance away from the cameras).

'The elephant in the room' slurred Hayden, too loudly, 'is that all straight men *are* attracted to fourteen year old girls.'

Maurice groped his face in disbelief. 'You're *such* a cunt' he groaned.

'Nah. Nah it's true' Hayden continued. 'But we all have the innate decency to not act on it.'

'That's just the fear of law breaking' said Maurice. 'It's not an innate decency embedded in all men.'

'Yes it is. We all break the law, all the time. It's more than that, it's respect. It's proof that human beings aren't the monsters we all were ten-thousand years ago.'

Jet Tea was effortlessly abstaining from this conversation. His face was placed firmly toward his phone, yet again. He chimed in, blissfully devoid of any context toward Maurice and Hayden's discussion.

'I think Jo 'The Hat' might be coming' he said.

'Erhn' grunted the others in reply.

'Yeah. She don't live that far away.'

'I thought she lives in Dalston?' said Maurice.

Jet Tea shrugged. 'London aint a big place, is it?'

'Trust me Maurice, you're breaking the law by drinking that beer' Hayden continued.

Maurice roared in frustration at Hayden's absurd conviction, and hurled his empty can away into the abyss of the train carriage. At that moment, the train stopped and opened its doors.

A tall, thin man in a long, beige jacket boarded the carriage, carrying a large black bag with what appeared to be a set of golf clubs protruding from its top. He had thin, mousy hair that seemed to be deliberately parted and one or two worry lines above his eyes. He looked about the place keenly, and then approached Maurice, Hayden and Jet Tea.

The three of them stopped what they were doing as he arrived, staring at him as he stood above Hayden and glanced curiously at his bag which was rested on the unoccupied seat next to him. The thin man's eyes remained on the bag for several seconds, and his face began to screw up into a frown.

'Yes?' Hayden sighed, trying hard to outdo his drunkenness and keep his head still.

'Erm' the man oozed condescendingly. 'Did your bag *pay* for that seat?'

The three of them stared about the empty carriage in disbelief. Maurice and Jet Tea looked at Hayden in anticipation of his response.

'Yes' he said. 'But the clumsy cunt went and lost his ticket.' His friends laughed.

The stranger huffed. 'I want to sit down' he said.

'Well there are plenty of seats' said Hayden, not quite believing the conversation he had become a part of.

'I want to sit *there*' said the man, gesturing to the seat upon which sat Hayden's bag. Hayden bit his lip. There was a momentary flame behind his eyes.

Maurice leant over. 'Leave it, mate' he semi-whispered. Hayden took a deep breath. He nodded in forfeit and then stood up, taking his bag with him as he approached a seat at the other end of the carriage. Jet Tea sighed a sigh of relief and he and Maurice also stood up and followed Hayden.

They sat down. Hayden once again placed the

bag in the seat beside him.

'Weird bastard' Maurice whispered.

'He needs to sort his life out' Jet Tea added, aping a conversationalist.

For a moment the three drunken friends sat in silence. Then that silence was broken from the other end of the carriage.

'*Eh hem*'. It was that man again. He'd stood up.

'Oh what the fuck now?' said Maurice under his breath. The man was approaching them again, dragging his big golf bag through the aisle. He arrived at their seating area and once again stood before Hayden, snarling at his bag.

'That's my seat' he sneered, nasally.

Hayden's rage reignited. He sized the man up. He was skinny, clearly upper-middle class and looked nearly twice his age. Probably hadn't been so much as kicked in the shins since he was thirteen. That would help to explain why he thought he could wax aggressively at a group of bewildered twenty-somethings without expectation of consequence. Hayden said nothing.

'*Move your bloody bag, you prick*' the man snarled in hierarchical tones. '*I'm a paying customer.*

I'm entitled to any bloody seat on this bloody train.' He was yelling at the top of his lungs now, waving authoritatively in every direction imaginable. Hayden looked on in disbelief.

Finally, the man leant in and grabbed Hayden's bag, shook it angrily and tossed it onto the carriage floor. That was enough.

The train began to slow. *'We Will Shortly be Arriving at Charing Cross'* said the kindly, automated female voice over the tannoy. That was their stop. That was more than enough.

Hayden shot out of his chair and on to his feet. Maurice and Jet Tea looked on. Seething and foaming at the mouth at the unbelievable nerve of this pompous invader, he lunged in and seized the man's golf bag. He pulled from it the first solid club he could find and unsheathed it furiously. In that moment he saw them all; all the condescending, suited customers at his bar who believed themselves above him because of the volume of their bank accounts; the power-crazed security guard who'd beaten his friend to a pulp; the policeman who sided with him; all of the friends and relatives who, despite knowing Hayden all his life and growing up with him, chose to immediately side with trained killers the moment he expressed an opinion. Unknowing victims of an imagined hierarchy, gutlessly treating him as the victim. His mind was hazy but his thoughts were clear. He saw them all in this cunt's contorting face, and he wanted them all to go away immediately.

The man gasped in horror and made a scared, sickly groan as the unfortunate reality of what he'd brought upon himself finally dawned on him. Hayden lifted the solid metal club high above his head and swung it violently toward the intruder, roaring in anger as he did so. The high-speed golf club impacted terribly upon the man's face with a deafening *crunch*, which brought him to his knees. The velocity of the affair had its consequences, principally of blood and incredible pain.

Hayden breathed heavily as he glared at the work of art that quivered at his feet. Right on cue, the train stopped completely and the doors opened once again.

'Let's go' said Hayden, flatly. He dropped the golf club and they each complied and departed the train, leaving the bloodied, whimpering man on the floor to continue his journey.

None of them were really *there*, any more. As they stomped drunkenly though the pattering rain of dark, West-end back streets even Jet Tea, who had been keeping a comparatively sober eye on his friends up until this point, was lost to his beer intake.

'You... can't eat... cheeseburgers and fucking... win games' Jet Tea shouted, staring confusedly at the reverse of his train ticket, which was adorned with a fast food voucher.

'You might be able to kill people-' he continued, laughing in Hayden's direction.

'Naagh, fucking it' Hayden barked. 'I be fine.'

'*Maaate*' laughed Maurice. 'You're in facking trouble.'

'Nagh' blabbed Hayden. ''How can they find me?'

'YOU!' Jet Tea suddenly shouted. 'YOU MAN!'

Maurice and Hayden looked dreamily up in the direction he was shouting. There was indeed a man, emerging from a pub on the corner across the road. He looked confused and concerned.

'Less go there' said Jet Tea. 'Issa pub.'

They were in the pub. The modest, weekday

clientele may or may not have been staring nervously at them as Maurice pounded the bar violently, demanding beer.

They were outside, somehow. Jet Tea was on the phone, covering his free ear with his hand in an attempt to maintain clarity against the noise, the rain and his state of mind. It was a familiar yet slightly unfamiliar voice. It was Jo 'The Hat.'

'In Charing Cross' Jet Tea mumbled.

'Yes you said' said the voice on the phone. '*Where* in Charing Cross?'

'The pub!'

'Stop saying that! Which pub?'

They were walking, again. Hayden was crying. Maurice was sure it was this way.

The room was dark, but alive. There was Jo 'The Hat'. Was she smiling or frowning? Jet Tea was happy.

Hayden was at the bar spending all the money he wasn't able to spend on bus fare earlier that day. Maurice stood in the centre of the dance floor. His fists were both raised triumphantly toward the ceiling. There was a considerable circular gap between him and the rest of the dance-floor occupants. Jet Tea squinted at his intrepid friend. What was the matter? His dancing wasn't particularly embarrassing or offensive. He wasn't dressed in a manner detrimental to the majority of the clientele, so why were most of his dance-floor neighbours looking so horrified at his dancing? Were they so judgmental? Were their collective perceptions of correct societal behaviour so caged-in by their hierarchy-dominated upbringings and educations that to simply behold the culturally incompatible sight of a solitary man enjoying music in an innocent manner was unbearable to them?

His cock was out.

That must have been it, thought Jet Tea as he observed Maurice's proud member bouncing about freely upon his gyrating frame, far above and beyond his crumpled trousers. The circle of space was widening as they beheld the flapping penis dancing smugly between the animated legs of its master. Large men in dark clothes were approaching.

Jo 'The Hat' looked angry. The music was too loud and everything was moving too quickly.

Maurice was being forced out by the large men. He was walking awkwardly because his fallen trousers were hindering his stride.

'YOU'RE ALL FUCKING PUSSIES!' He yelled. 'FUCK YOU ALL!'

Jet Tea was bent double, laughing intensely. Jo 'The Hat' was shaking her head in frustration.

'He's a dick!' she was yelling above the incomprehensible music.

'He's the legend that is Maurice' laughed Jet Tea.

Jo 'The Hat' groaned. Jet Tea danced seductively toward her. She frowned and stepped back.

He said something unrepeatable about his conviction that she 'wanted him'. And that was most certainly it.

'I was never even interested in you!' she screamed. 'Go fuck yourself!'

'You just don't get it!' he screeched. 'Because you're BORING!'

Jo 'The Hat' winced in disgust and stormed out.

'No way' said the cab driver. 'I'm not taking him.'

'Put your fucking trousers on' cried Jet Tea,

soaking from the pounding rain.

'These cunts don't get it' Maurice babbled righteously as they hurtled past Central London's tired sights. 'When me and my cock met, it was like a meeting of minds. It was like... fucking... Simon and Garfunkel. You lot have never known a more perfect partnership. Me and my cock, man. Me and my cock forever.'

Jet Tea wasn't listening. He was singing something almost indescribable that sounded vaguely like *Debaser* by The Pixies in a pitch that neither Maurice nor Hayden had been able to reach since primary school and banging the windows to a beat.

'AH HA HA HO!' Sang Jet Tea. 'CHAN AN LOOSER! AH HA HA HO!' He drummed on the window.

'Me and my cock are the fucking Lennon and McCartney of the twenty-first fucking century' yelled Maurice. Jet Tea's singing continued. Hayden was weeping into his hands, saying 'I'm fucked. I'm fucked.'

It was rumoured that the cab driver retired shortly after.

Hayden had been dropped home first, and now Maurice and Jet Tea stood in the pouring rain outside the latter's house, swaying and occasionally tripping over nothing.

'I love you mate' said Maurice, and in that fit of drunken, teary-eyed passion, Jet Tea leapt upon his friend and gave him a bear-hug like the best Christmas jumper any grandmother could give. At that moment Maurice jerked his head back and seemed to rush unwillingly out of his spot, through some kind of white-hot, spiky void, as though contact with Jet Tea had caused him to do so.

When, seconds later, he resurfaced, he was no longer standing in the dark, wet street outside Jet Tea's house. Jet Tea and the cab were nowhere to be seen. No, Maurice was now walking down a somewhat straight, narrow street. His head was clear once again, he felt like he hadn't touched alcohol in years. It was early evening. The sky was dusty-blue, but the buildings he passed were familiar; row-upon-row of near-identical, early Victorian terraces, laid out on a vast grid of linear streets that Maurice explored aimlessly. There was a faint, perpetual lingering mist about the place, or at least there seemed to be.

Maurice recognised it now. It was Soho; what

should have been the bustling heart of London's west end but was in this case desolate, eerie and ruined. The buildings looked ever more tired than usual and all of the windows were either boarded up or broken and untreated. Signs of shops and restaurants were as faded as to being mostly unintelligible. It was quite obvious that Maurice had been the first to tread here in decades.

A fleeting thought struck him. Had he finally done it? Finally succeeded in destroying London as he'd so often jovially claimed was his intention? Was it achieved on that very night with the illusion of time passed merely a testament to his destructive achievements? Probably not. He was sure he heard Jet Tea's distant giggle somewhere.

As he continued to wander the dead, labyrinthine side-streets Maurice became certain that things were staring at him, but from where? Not the empty windows as would have been obvious. It made him feel uneasy as he turned endless corners into indistinguishable streets, not knowing what he was looking for but ever more frustrated that he couldn't find it.

He looked up at the sky. It seemed closer, somehow, like the atmosphere was a book that was closing.

Maurice knew he was within seconds of shrinking out of being as the sky drew nearer. At that moment he became aware of another staring at him. Not malevolently, like before, but with kindness. A long shadow fell on the broken cobbles and without even looking, Maurice knew it was her. Then suddenly the imminent and unstoppable death of the world felt absolutely fine, because she was there.

That remained the only event Maurice would properly recall from that night, and it probably didn't even happen.

Little more remained in the grasp of Jet Tea's memory. He awoke among more pain than his recent years had known. The golf club, Maurice's cock and Jo 'The Hat'. Those were all the elements he required to assure himself that he'd made a colossal mess. He never heard from Jo 'The Hat', or indeed her friend Jessica, ever again.

The Mental Girl

On weekday evenings, Jet Tea and Hayden tended to forego the Treaty and instead drink in the more laid back Three Tuns. The Three Tuns was a nicer, smaller pub that sat on the high street and was a particularly pleasant place to go of a milder evening if there was an outside table free and it wasn't raining. They often found themselves people watching and forming a running commentary.

They would occasionally visit The Three Tuns on weekend binges, say for a four-pint starter or if the preceding week had offered events severe enough to be discussed over beer (the Treaty was seldom quiet enough to accommodate a serious conversation). However,

Maurice and the Tuns' landlord didn't really get on ever since Maurice threw a pumpkin through the window on his birthday, so he often urged his friends not to stay too long.

On this evening Maurice was out of town and Jet Tea and Hayden were sat outside The Three Tuns having a quiet pint and observing the varying degrees of passer-by. Jet Tea seemed relatively serene given the recent demolition of his chances with Jo 'The Hat' (whom he didn't once mention, although he did briefly speak of a pretty red-headed girl he'd met the other night who, in his words, 'loved him').

Hayden's mobile phone rang. The display read 'Unknown Number', but he could hazard a guess as to who it may have been. He hung up and raised a hand to his creased, worried forehead.

'Look at that girl' said Jet Tea, nodding toward the high street in general.

'What girl?' replied Hayden.

Jet Tea didn't reply, he simply nodded again and gestured meekly with his hand. Hayden looked again, there was indeed a girl; rather young looking with short-cut blonde hair. She was laughing to herself in the high street and seemed to be spinning slowly for no visible reason. A short distance from her, though close enough to indicate they were in fact acquainted, stood two men. One looked some years older than her, while the other seemed to be close to her age. Her father and brother, Hayden decided.

The two men were smiling at the young woman amiably, but there was a kind of tiredness to their smiles, as though they were enduring something long and unrelenting. Jet Tea hadn't actually noticed either of the men in the scenario.

Hayden raised an eyebrow. 'What about her?' he asked.

'She's…' Jet Tea hesitated. 'Interesting.'

'Yep.'

'There's something quite sexy about her' Jet Tea continued, almost entranced by her slow spinning and the fact that she didn't seem to remotely care about who was watching her. Hayden leant back in his chair slightly and breathed in through his nose.

'What?' he asked in disbelief.

'I don't know. She's attractive in a way that she's a bit weird and doesn't seem to care. I like girls like that.'

'Mate' said Hayden earnestly. 'Are you being serious?'

'What?'

'Do you know what you're looking at?'

'What?'

Hayden sighed. 'She's mental.'

'So?' said Jet Tea, 'everyone's a bit mental.'
He was not wrong.

'No, no' said Hayden. 'I mean she's properly
mental, as in she doesn't know what's going on at all.'

Jet Tea one-upped Hayden and raised both
eyebrows as he suddenly realised what Hayden, in less
articulate terms, had meant to say; the young lady was in
fact severely mentally handicapped. She was not
spinning and laughing because she thought it would be a
bit of silly fun, she was doing so because her
consciousness had been, for whatever reason, removed
from any that can be reconciled with real-world
rationality and was continually telling her that this was
standard behaviour incarnate and she may continue to go
about it with no qualms.

'Sorry, what?'

'Look at her, Jet Tea!' Hayden almost shouted.
'She's handicapped. That's her family with her, look at
how they're sort of letting her get on with it but
maintaining a concerned closeness. They've quite
clearly just let her out for the day, she has absolutely no
control over what she's doing, or her dad and brother

218

wouldn't need to look after her.'

'Are you sure?'

Jet Tea rested his elbows upon the table, pressed his fingers together and leant forward, almost squinting at the girl. She had stopped spinning and was now sort of wobbling back to her family, her mouth ajar. Her father was smiling at her through clenched lips. Jet Tea snorted a small giggle.

'Oh yeah' he laughed.

Hayden also laughed, but it was a laugh that lay somewhere between nervousness and relief. 'Do you realise now?'

The grinning face of Jet Tea turned slowly toward Hayden. 'Yeah I see what you mean' he said.

'You're mental, Jet Tea' Hayden joked.

But Jet Tea had already turned back to the girl. By now she was walking -with apparent difficulty-away, each hand holding one of her companions' hands. Jet Tea would not take his eyes off her. It wasn't that he was still trying to work out if Hayden was wrong or right; he had already realised that the girl was indeed mentally ill to a degree above and beyond himself. What Jet Tea was actually doing was trying to force himself to not be interested in her now that he had come to realise this. All his instinctive senses of decency and proper societal consciousness were telling him that he shouldn't be attracted to this person's behaviour. Unfortunately his conscious mind was telling him otherwise. He continued to stare until her departing form had disappeared from view. Then he tried to outdo his sight limitations and follow her down the street with his eyes. If only he could just know one more thing about her.

His stare was so transfixed on one point that all things surrounding that point began to obscure and fade until there was only the pathway that she had walked down. All the figures, silhouetted by streetlamps, had dispersed into incomprehensible shadow and all buildings were curtained by the dark blue night sky. Jet Tea's eyes now simply beheld a yellow-lit cobbled pathway, piercing a desolate, dark void and stretching faraway until it was consumed by shadow. A distant voice said his name; it was Hayden, who was supposed to be sitting opposite him at the same table but for some reason had moved to a distant location, the furthest allowable point for his voice to be still faintly heard.

Jet Tea shook himself out of the trance, and for anyone else that would have been the moment when all the senses were back to normal. For Jet Tea the hypnotic void remained. The sky, which was well within his periphery all that time, had somehow become a deep-red without having undergone any visible change. The vanishing point of the solitary pathway was drawing closer while the individual cobbles that it consisted of appeared to gradually drift away. Before long, there was no pathway.

He looked round at Hayden, now a distant silhouette drifting slowly backwards, limbs completely motionless. The sky was purple now.

Jet Tea had completed the process of regaining his senses and somehow knew exactly what to do. He extended his left arm and opened his hand, ready to grip something. A faraway object hurtled with incredible speed towards him. As it drew rapidly closer it glinted in the changing light of the colourful sky. Before long it was close enough to be identifiable as a half-full (or perhaps half-empty) pint glass. It shot closer and smacked perfectly into Jet Tea's grip, stopping suddenly. In an instant the mundane shapes of reality clapped around it with a sound not unlike that of a child finishing a milkshake.

The sky was dark-blue again, Hayden was two feet away and all the buildings were where they should have been, which was a relief because at that exact moment Jet Tea decided he needed a stronger drink.

Hayden was smiling. 'You alright mate?'

'Yeah' said Jet Tea, not entirely sure what he was responding to. 'Hayden,'

'Yes?'

'Drink vodka with me.'

Craig

Jet Tea's vodka hangover was less than welcome. Even so, he'd managed to endure a day's work; ten solid hours of dipping frozen chips in and out of the fryer, listening to the same twelve chart tracks again and again on tinny loop through a tattered, portable CD player and the nauseating guffaws of Joe and Glen following their repeated, inspired decisions to refer to him as 'Harry Potter.'

He'd even resisted the urge to antagonise them by requesting to listen to his Blur CD. This job was becoming increasingly trying. The work itself was, if possible, getting easier. The willingness to actually turn up wasn't.

After work he darted, quickly as possible, to The Good Yarn. Jet Tea almost never visited the pub by himself, but on this evening he couldn't fathom not going. Never was a pint or five so essential as on this evening. Perhaps he'd meet someone interesting. Maybe that nice, red-headed graphic artist he met the other night would turn up. An evening that begins lonely doesn't necessarily need to end that way.

He purchased a pint of lager and, clutching it, turned away from the bar. What to do now? Jet Tea was unsure of how to behave in a pub by himself. He'd seen older gentlemen do it so deftly, but what was the minimum acceptable age to be solitary in a public house and not look out of place? Jet Tea suspected he'd not quite reached it, whatever it was. He turned back to the bar and leant upon it, sipping his beer and flashing uncertain glances about the place. At one point he caught the eye of a pretty barmaid and, in an effort to keep it, raised his eyebrows and bit his lip in a vague grin. She looked away as politely as could be achieved.

This wasn't enjoyable, he thought. It was supposed to be a relaxing, solitary, post-work pint. Instead, Jet Tea felt too self-conscious and aware of his unsettling surroundings to really relax and enjoy his own company. He'd have to finish the beer promptly and rethink his evening.

Then it happened.

Jet Tea instinctively reacted to the modest creak of the pub door opening and, bereft of something better to do, looked around. There was Gemma, heading a small army of female friends into the room. They seemed to be mid-conversation and laughing heartily at something. Gemma. He hadn't seen her in a while. She'd never replied to his texts, acknowledged receipt of his favourite unread novel or explained what the bloody hell she was doing with that man that night behind the Treaty. Now here she was, about to socially collide with her formative suitor, who'd been reduced to nursing a solitary lager at the dark end of a miserable bar in an unremarkable chain pub that was likely only an interval on her vastly superior night.

What would he do? She looked more beautiful than he'd remembered, and the memory of all those wonderful, optimistic feelings he'd felt before began to creep back. He'd felt so young then, before she bowed out of his life and made way for the tragedy that was Jo 'The Hat'. It had only been a few weeks, but he felt old and miserable recalling them.

Glugging the remainder of his drink, he dropped

clumsily from his bar stool and skidded for the toilet. The last time he darted so frantically to a pub toilet he'd met Gemma shortly after. This odd symmetry gave him hope for some reason.

He took refuge in a cubicle and pulled out his phone to call Maurice. Maurice would save him, as he always did.

'Hello?' Maurice answered.

'Alright mate' said Jet Tea. 'Fancy coming for a drink?'

'Treaty?'

'No, Good Yarn.'

'Why are you there?' asked Maurice.

'Don't know' said Jet Tea. 'I just felt like it, for a change.'

Maurice paused for a moment. 'Yeah, why not?' he said.

Success. Jet Tea clenched his fist in triumph without realising it. 'See you in a bit then' he said, before hanging up.

After flushing the toilet, so as to give the impression to possible occupants of the same room that he had a valid reason for being there, Jet Tea strolled back into the pub. As he emerged he saw the door open from across the room and Maurice arrived. That was rather swift, thought Jet Tea. It didn't matter, he was here. They acknowledged each other and met at the bar.

'Is that Gemma?' Maurice asked, nodding in her direction. 'Is that who you're with?'

Jet Tea bit his lip. 'No, I was on my own. Yes that's Gemma.'

Maurice sighed. 'Is that why you called me?' he asked.

'What?' cried Jet Tea, 'you're a mate! I just wanted to see my old mate Maurice!' With that remark he poked Maurice on the arm repeatedly. 'Now let's go and say hello.'

They made their way over to where Gemma and her friends were sitting. They seemed to be constantly enjoying that hearty conversation, but Gemma's smile drooped ever so slightly when she saw Jet Tea approach.

'Jet Tea' she said, blankly. 'How are you?'

Her soft Scottish accent danced and lilted through his head as she spoke. He'd missed her voice, he realised.

'Not bad thanks' he replied. 'Haven't seen you in the Treaty for a while.'

'Yeah I stopped going there because y-' she trailed off. 'I don't like it there any more.'

Maurice sat down without invitation. His eyes

darted briefly over Gemma's group of friends. There were three of them, excluding her. They all seemed to be about Gemma's age, none particularly presented themselves as being potentially interesting. Jet Tea sat down next to Maurice. He then proceeded to say and do absolutely nothing. Maurice winced at his friend as he beheld his glum frown, clenched fingers and unmoving body language. It was at times like this that Jet Tea's lack of female attention failed to surprise him, and his modest history of it rather did. If Jet Tea ever found love again, Maurice would concede that magic was real.

After a moment's awkward silence, Gemma returned to her friends. Their conversation dropped in volume slightly but probably wasn't worth scrutinising any way, Maurice assumed. After a while she pulled something from her hand bag. It was a book. Jet Tea, noticing it also, almost shot up out of his seat, his blank expression contorting into one of hope. The book was an average sized paperback; a bit run-down on the spine and its pages were yellowing.

'What's that?' Maurice asked.

Gemma looked around, visibly wondering what he and Jet Tea were doing at the table. She answered nonetheless.

'*Les Miserables*' she said. 'A friend gave me it

as a present.'

'Was that Shaun?' asked one of her friends; a tall, dark-haired girl who looked like she may have had some Asian heritage.

Gemma failed to suppress a smile. 'Yes' she beamed. Her friends became animated with glee at this. Maurice noticed Jet Tea's expression becoming increasingly sour. He squinted at the volume Gemma held in her hands.

'Did you say that's *Les Miserables*?' he asked.

'Yes' she replied. 'The novel.'

Maurice nodded. 'How long is it, out of interest?'

'Why?'

'Just wondering.'

Gemma huffed and flicked through the book. 'Three-hundred and twelve pages' she said.

Maurice paused. 'That's the abridged version.'

Gemma also paused. 'Sorry?'

'Yeah' Maurice continued. '*Les Miserables* is about a thousand pages long. It's an epic, historical novel' he reached over and took the book from Gemma's hands. 'See? It says here, "Abridged."'

Gemma sat in silence for a moment. 'So?'

'Who got it for you?' asked Maurice.

'Just a friend' she replied.

'He thinks you're stupid' said Maurice.

'I'm sorry?'

'He thinks you're an idiot.'

Gemma's friend with the dark hair and possibly Asian features leant in. 'What makes you think that?' she asked sternly.

'Because it's abridged!' cried Maurice. 'Look, this edition wouldn't cost much less than the complete volume, especially second-hand, so it's hardly an issue of money. He made a judgment call, whether consciously or not, to get you the shorter version of the novel. He clearly believes the full version would be too much for you.'

'He might not have realised' said the dark-haired girl.

'Maybe not, but he'd have had a careful look at it before handing it over. Or at least apologised for accidentally getting the wrong edition, which I'm guessing he didn't, as Gemma has only just found out it's abridged.'

'I'm not an idiot!' Gemma protested.

'I'm certain you're not' replied Maurice. 'That's beside the point. Your friend... Shane?'

'Shaun.'

'Shaun obviously thinks you are.'

Nobody said any more on the subject. Gemma half-heartedly took the book from Maurice, glanced at it and dropped it on the table. Something had been shattered.

Maurice shot a grin in Jet Tea's direction. He looked happier than he did a few minutes ago.

'Sorry' said the half-Asian girl in an unapologetic tone, 'what's your name?'

'Maurice. I'm Jet Tea's best mate.'

'And that's Jet Tea, is it?' she asked, gesturing in the direction of the correct answer.

'It is.' Jet Tea's silence was beginning to irritate Maurice. He'd come out to save Jet Tea and had won him a rather spectacular victory, yet he wasn't upping his efforts.

'My name is Annie' she said, suddenly cheerier.

'Nice to meet you' said Maurice. 'So you've only just met Jet Tea, have you? The way he talks about Gemma I'd assumed he'd be well acquainted with all her friends by now.'

'I've heard of him' she said, staring tiredly over at Gemma.

'Few haven't' Maurice replied.

Jet Tea sat staring into the group, slowly sipping

his beer. He'd winced when Maurice mentioned how often he talked about Gemma. How could he? It wasn't even true. He barely spoke of her. A brash, nasal announcement caused him to jump out of his seat and choke ever-so-slightly on his mouthful.

'Alright, ladies and gents' it said.

The population of the table spun in the voice's direction. There stood a tall, well-tanned young man with effortlessly styled hair and a tight, beige shirt that loyally boasted of how much time its owner spent in the gym. He was clutching a small glass of cola (presumably with vodka or whiskey in it) and wearing a grin that Maurice decided he didn't like, for some reason.

'Hello' said Maurice.

'You lot having a private moment, then?' asked the new arrival.

Gemma smiled. 'No.'

'That's nice' he said, moving in to sit down. 'Mind if I sit down?'

'Not at all' said Annie.

A second or two of silence then followed. Maurice broke it.

'So do you lot know this guy?' he asked.

Annie shook her head. 'I don't' she said.

'Me neither' said one of Gemma's other friends.

'Now now' the man oozed at Maurice. 'Two blokes, four birds, can't have a go at me for levelling out the numbers a bit, eh?'

Gemma laughed. Annie glanced skeptically over at Maurice, who raised his eyebrows in return. Jet Tea frowned. Gemma's other friends hid their smiles behind their drinks glasses.

'I'm Craig' he grinned. He leant over and shook each of their hands enthusiastically.

'Gemma' she replied as he took her hand, seeming to clutch it marginally longer than the others. 'This is Annie, Amy and Sarah.'

'Hi' said Craig, nodding. 'And how about your two lovely gentleman friends?' he asked.

Maurice introduced himself and Jet Tea.

'Pleasure' said Craig. 'I've just got off work, thought I'd pop in for a quick one.'

The next question hacked violently at Maurice's throat as he found it escaping him.

'What do you do?'

He hated asking it, and only ever did so when in such fruitless company simply as a means to keep silence at bay. He would have left the moment this smug bastard had joined them, as Jet Tea was offering nothing,

233

but he had an inkling things could go somewhere interesting with Annie, so he remained.

'I'm a copy writer for a large high street firm' Craig replied. Maurice didn't care. As far as he was concerned, if someone's defining characteristic is where they spend the first eight hours of their weekdays, then they mustn't have much else going for them. The more unusual and admirable one's interests, the more they define you. Nobody is introduced as 'so-and-so who likes *X Factor* and KFC'.

Gemma, Amy and Sarah nodded with genuine interest. Jet Tea shrugged and let out a small, condescending giggle at the floor. Craig momentarily glared at him. 'And how about yourself?' he asked Maurice.

'I'm a musician, primarily' he replied.

'What do you mean "primarily"?' asked Craig.

'I'm sorry?'

'Well, it's either your job' he said sternly, 'or just something you enjoy doing. I don't go around introducing myself as "Craig Tully: beer drinker."'

'Rhymes with drinker' mumbled Jet Tea.

'Is that a hobby that's on par with being a musician?' asked Maurice.

Craig laughed. 'I get where you're coming

from' he said. 'But is it your job, or what?'

Maurice leant forward. 'I'm not sure what you mean by "job", to be honest.'

'Well do you do it for a living? My job pays twenty-eight grand a year, after tax. I own my own flat in Kensal Rise and get five weeks paid holiday.'

'I get by.'

Craig scanned Maurice, top to bottom, then bit his lip. 'Fair enough' he said, pretending to try and suppress a giggle.

'Well' Maurice continued. 'Any musician will tell you. Sometimes it pays, sometimes it doesn't. One week I might take home a hundred quid for half an hour's work, the next I might barely scrape my bus fare. It doesn't matter too much, because I fucking love doing it.'

'But you can't exactly live like that, can you?' Craig replied. 'You're a grown man. Don't you have something more secure on the side?'

'Occasionally' said Maurice. 'But what does being grown up have to do with what I enjoy doing for a living?'

'Don't say "for a living"' barked Craig. 'It's an insult to people who do proper work.'

'What, like you?' laughed Maurice.

Craig opened his mouth, presumably to excrete a condescending response, but Maurice didn't let him.

'Your obvious understanding of what makes someone grown up is subjective. I'm happy with what I do, where I live, who I spend time with and what I do with my spare time. That, to me, says grown up, because whether you believe me or not, I'm at peace with the person I am. You bowled into this room uninvited, introduced yourself with a job title and then had a go at me for not having the exact same life as you.'

Craig chose to ignore the majority of what Maurice had said. He appealed to Gemma and her friends. '"Uninvited"' he repeated. 'Does anyone else have a problem with me being here?'

Nobody committed to a proper answer. Jet Tea mumbled something miserably then laughed.

'Thank you' said Craig, smugly. 'I think you need to double check "grown up" in the dictionary.'

'I'm sure it'll say "smug cunt with a haircut"' said Jet Tea, quietly. He looked at Gemma; she was enthralled in this heated conversation. She hadn't shot him a glance since Craig had arrived.

'In my dictionary' said Maurice, 'it reads "a term invented by conventional society to extinguish free-spirits"'.

Craig burst into laughter, Amy and Sarah joined him. 'Your dictionary?' he turned to Annie. 'Is this guy a dick?' he asked in a manner that implied he did not urgently require an answer.

'No' she replied stoically. Maurice smiled.

'I thought you were a dick when I first met you' said Gemma.

'But not now?' Maurice replied.

Gemma grinned. 'Nah,'

'Then that just means you're a poor judge of character. You thinking I'm a dick before you know me properly is your shortcoming, not mine. I haven't changed.'

'Alright' said Gemma, annoyed. 'I said I like you now. Christ.'

Maurice, with the aged conviction that only young men possess and Craig, with the disgusting closed-mindedness of someone who has never even toyed with the idea of leaving their bubble, continued to argue, while Jet Tea looked on helplessly.

'You can't expect an entire species to agree to live by a relatively recent set of societal ideals' said Maurice. 'We're animals, at the end of the day and animals are notorious for doing whatever they want.'

'We are not animals' said Craig. 'We're people.

We can't be both.'

'What?' said Maurice, confused. 'What do you mean we can't? Lions are animals *and* lions, aren't they? What the fuck are you talking about?'

Annie laughed at this. Craig leant over and tapped Maurice on the shoulder in a patronising manner. 'I think our friend would rather go and live with the lions' he said, grinning widely at the female population of the table.

After a while the argument fizzled down to a discussion. Craig eventually left the table to purchase more drinks. Maurice had since fallen into an enthusiastic conversation with Annie. Suddenly, Gemma turned to Jet Tea.

'Oh by the way' she said, causing Jet Tea to snap out of his misanthropic trance. 'I forgot to say thanks for the book.'

He paused. This was unexpected, and as such he'd failed to arm himself with ready responses. He'd have to improvise.

'No worries' he replied. 'It's my favourite book.'

Gemma smiled. 'I like it too. I've read it before, but I never had my own copy, so thank you.'

'That's alright.' A pause followed. 'Maurice and your mate seem to be getting on.'

'Oh, aye' said Gemma. 'But nothing's going to happen.'

'Really?' replied Jet Tea, unable to reconcile this announcement with Maurice's track-record. 'He's pretty good at what he does.'

'Annie has a boyfriend' said Gemma. 'They're in love.'

'Really?'

'Yeah. His name's Danny, he has no legs. They've been together for years.'

Jet Tea looked over at Maurice. 'Shot down for a guy with no legs' he said. 'Aint that a kick in the teeth.'

Gemma frowned. 'That was mean.'

'Sorry.'

'I'll forgive you.'

Craig returned with a tray of shots. As if by coincidence, Gemma and Jet Tea's conversation ceased.

Annie looked up at the tray. 'Careful' she said. 'Gemma can't handle her drink.'

'She's Scottish' scoffed Craig. 'She can't handle her not-drink'.

The dreaded final bell sounded. The lights went up and after some drunken resistance the last of the customers were ushered out into the night.

'Where are we off to now?' Craig slurred. 'Any good clubs open?'

Maurice sidled up to Annie. 'I think we're going to head off, to be honest.' Annie nodded and looked sheepishly at Gemma.

Gemma's jaw dropped through inebriated astonishment. 'What about Danny?' she cried.

'Just leave it' said Annie. 'I'll talk to you tomorrow.' With that, she and Maurice departed.

Craig turned to Jet Tea. 'How about you, little man? What are you up to now?'

Jet Tea grimaced and turned away. 'Might go and buy some hair gel and a pink shirt. Fit in.'

Craig laughed, but looked bewildered. 'What did you say?'

'Fuck it' said Jet Tea.

'No, what did you say, you little cunt?' Craig was no longer laughing, and a dark anger had shrouded his features.

'Leave it Craig' pleaded Gemma.

'Don't think I haven't been paying attention to your snidey wanker little remarks you little prick.'

He was approaching now. The gravity of Jet Tea's earlier hostility had begun to dawn on him and he cowered back in vain. Through all the self-satisfaction and grooming, he had failed to notice how big Craig was. Those gym-toned muscles bulging through the fabric of his shirt were now more apparent than ever as his quarry loomed. Craig lumbered over to Jet Tea and, screaming in fury, swung an almighty fist at him, cracking him hard on the nose. Jet Tea stumbled back and cried out, grabbing his face in agony. Where was Maurice now? Why wasn't he more thankful before, when his friend had saved him?

'And my shirt is beige, you cunt!' Craig shouted, spreading his arms to demonstrate how much further damage he could easily do, or at least to reiterate the actual colour of his shirt.

'Leave him alone!' Gemma yelled, grabbing Craig, who eventually stepped back. Jet Tea felt a droplet of warm blood trickle down his top lip. He tasted its unwelcome, metallic tang as he looked upon Craig, foaming and willing to attack again.

'That fucking wormy little wanker aint even worth it' he snarled, retreating. 'Snotty little kids thinking they can speak to me like that. I'll fucking break your skinny little neck next time!'

Jet Tea felt tiny. He wanted so much to impress Gemma, and here she was latched onto the arm of a bigger, better man, pleading with him not to harm a child. How was he so miniscule to her? Barely an hour ago they were embroiled in a loving conversation about literature. Intellectual equals. Now he was a runt, being spared from extermination by pity only.

Craig turned to depart, and Gemma stepped back with him. Surely she wasn't going to go home with him?

Amy and Sarah stood by, unsettled by the incident. 'Gemma, we're off' said Sarah, and they quickly left.

'Gemma?' Jet Tea cried.

She was fast departing. 'Erm, I'll see you soon, Jet Tea.' She said.

This was unbearable. The beast that had just attempted to crush him was now taking the love of his life away. Jet Tea watched helplessly as they shrunk into the shadow of the night. He barely resisted the urge to claw the ensuing image from his eyes. He pictured him, pummeling her violently in the twilit warmth of his flat in Kensal Rise, her relatively helpless frame rocking along involuntarily with his rhythm. Then, clutching her scalp dominantly as she pleasured him. He pictured her smile, and for the first time it made him want to vomit.

What could he do? Throw himself under that oncoming lorry? Too much. Just go to sleep? No, he might dream. There was only one other option. He looked northward. The distant glow of the Treaty shone back at him over the no-man's-land of the desolate high street, beckoning him in from the cold despair. There was only one place left to go. But after that? Maybe it was time to leave this place for good.

Alice

Hayden worked in a pub. That means several things when compared to the standard working life of a nine-to-fiver; lie-ins (and lock-ins) are so common that the novelty quickly wears off, a weekend can begin on a Tuesday morning, a lunch break can occur at 9.30 pm and a working day can end at 2 am if it so wishes. On this evening it did just that. It wasn't one of the pubs he and his friends drank in, but a posh one frequented by office monkeys. After nine and a half hours of running up and down a slippery bar, scrutinised by the pompous elite and at the beck and call of a flapping twenty pound note twixt the sticky fingers of a suited, condescending snob with his eyes in his nostrils, Hayden just wanted to fall into his mattress and assimilate with it for eternity.

He stood at the far end of the bus stop, leaning against the post that displays the time-table and what buses one can actually get from there, waiting patiently. His phone rang; he looked at the screen and grimaced, hanging up. Not long now. Joining him were a middle-aged drunk man periodically kicking the ground and mumbling through the frustration of waiting, a slightly younger gentlemen, somewhat intimidated by the drunk man and pretending to use his phone in a desperate attempt to ensure he was ignoring him as much as possible and, oh dear. Someone Hayden knew.

By-and-large a deliberately anti-social young man, Hayden rather cherished his bus journeys to and from work and secretly considered them spoiled whenever the bus was shared by someone he knew personally. For this meant a compulsory conversation, and bus journeys were considered by Hayden to be the last little bits of 'me-time' before a long shift, sleep or friends. He'd much prefer to listen to music, stare into space or read whatever book he was reading than to have to make small talk with somebody just because they were there. And yet, after a nine and a half hour shift, here was Alice, a friend of a friend that Hayden had perhaps had three short conversations with in the year since he'd met her. Of course she would naturally initiate a pointless conversation about nothing, and each of the participants would be too polite to cut it short or to choose not to sit beside the other.

Perhaps Hayden could dart up to the top deck before Alice noticed him.

The bus arrived and Alice had still not registered Hayden's presence, so Hayden decided to put his plan into action. He was the first to step on (years of getting two to four buses a day left him with the natural ability to predict exactly where the front doors of the bus would stop), beeped his Oyster card on the reader, nodded politely at the driver and bounded upstairs, where he parked himself in the front, right-hand seat. The front, right-hand seat is the best seat on the bus. It is beside two windows and, thanks to it being directly in front of the staircase, there are no seats in front of or behind it. It is the closest one can get to a private booth on a London bus, and Hayden had just successfully acquired it for his journey home. The closest fellow passenger, an odd-looking chap with most of his face buried behind facial hair, was two seats away. Success.

Alice felt the same way about that particular seat.

The evening had been rather unkind to Alice, who now wanted nothing more than to sit peacefully on the bus, listen to her music and go home to bed. She'd had three pints of cider and was in that groggy, contemplative mood that directly precedes tipsiness. The bus arrived and, having not picked out the best part of the bus stop, she was to be the third passenger on board. All she could do was hope that nobody else desired that seat.

Hayden slouched back into the seat; he was so low that the top of his head did not appear over the top of it.

Alice climbed the stairs and as her desired seat appeared empty, she was hopeful. Her hopes were dashed as she then reached her destination to find that that dark-haired lad with the big coat had gotten there first.

Then she noticed who it was. Their eyes met, it was too late now for Alice to sit elsewhere.

'Alright?' said Hayden with an admirably convincing smile.

'Hello' replied Alice. 'I'm not bad thanks, how are you?'

Their dialogue could have been ripped word-for-word from *A Beginner's Guide to a Standard, Pointless Conversation*, except that book doesn't exist.

'I'm alright. You off home?' asked Hayden.

'Yeah. You?'

'Yeah. Just been at work. What have you been up to?'

'I was just at the Treaty' said Alice.

'Oh right, good night?'

Alice suddenly remembered exactly who Hayden was, which should ideally occur at the start of a conversation but there you go. Hayden was friends with Jet Tea.

'You know Jet Tea, don't you?' The tone of her voice, as well as the mere mention of Jet Tea's name, told Hayden that the conversation would at least be an interesting, if not particularly happy, one.

'Yeah, why?' he asked.

'He was out tonight.'

'Oh yes, I was going to join him, but I had to work. Did you speak to him?'

'Yes.' That one word managed to tell Hayden a lot of things, and they weren't very good.

Despite having predicted the answer, Hayden then asked; 'How was he?'

The bus had begun to move, there was no escape from this conversation.

'He's being a fucking dick.'

Being said Alice. That wasn't good, that

249

implies she wasn't actually over whatever she went through that night. Jet Tea can't be *being* a dick to her; he's not here, thought Hayden. He felt the odd-looking chap close to them was listening to their conversation, for some reason.

Hayden remained diplomatic. 'Oh yeah? What's he done?'

'We met not long ago,' she replied. Hayden recalled this, Jet Tea talking with enthusiasm about the kooky, redheaded graphic artist he met. His exact words, if Hayden recalled correctly, were 'She Loves Me.'

'I knew he liked me then but I've never done anything to make him think I like him in that way.'

Hayden bit his lip as Alice sighed and continued.

'We swapped numbers' she said, 'but as friends. Just as friends, because I thought he was a nice enough guy and that. So he's been texting me every now and again, and it's all been nice enough, so I've replied.'

First mistake, thought Hayden. Being a female and showing anything approaching attention to Jet Tea is bad enough. Giving him your number and texting him, even in reply, is just asking for trouble.

'But then he started texting more and more, and

he was obviously annoyed that it wasn't going anywhere so he starts asking me these serious questions, like if I have a boyfriend and why I'm ignoring him. I wasn't even ignoring him!'

'He's just been through a tough break-up.'

Alice ignored that remark. 'He needs to back off' she said. 'So tonight I was with my friend Rick. We were sat together, and your friend was just sitting there staring at me from the other table. It was really uncomfortable.'

'That sounds about right' said Hayden, trying to be as impartial as possible.

'Then he obviously decided to give up and left' said Alice.

'That's alright then, isn't it?' asked Hayden.

'But when he walked past me he said something like "time to go and jump under a bus", and laughed.'

'Ah.'

'I don't know what he thinks he's going to get out of acting like that, he's not going to get me to like him.'

Hayden glanced at the window; the nightly sights of his homeward journey passed by. Iceland. The Wishing Well pub. Amir Food and Wine. That block of flats he'd been beaten up outside of when he was fourteen. Home needed to hurry up and arrive. This conversation was destroying his bus journey.

'Jet Tea has been going through a lot lately,' said Hayden. 'And he has a lot of emotional issues as it is.'

'Yeah' said Alice with nothing but venom, apparently taking Hayden's last comment to mean 'He's just a complete wanker who deserves no sympathy at all.' Hayden glanced at her with resentment. Just another unfeeling party who can't comprehend why his tragic situation could possibly be as upsetting to Jet Tea as it is to them.

The park. The Prince of Wales Pub. The small Tesco. The bucket shop.

'I'll have a word' said Hayden as he stood up and pressed the stop button, stopping this conversation.

'No' said Alice. 'Don't bother, I can't be dealing with him as it is.'

'Alright I'll tell him to stop harassing people then, I won't mention your name.'

'Yeah okay' said Alice. 'Do that.'

'Selfish wanker' said Hayden.

'Yeah. See you soon.'

Hayden nodded a good-bye and disappeared down the stairs as the bus slowed. Alice now had her favourite seat. The odd-looking chap got up to alight also.

As he stood on the dark street and watched the bus depart, Hayden repeated to himself; 'Selfish wanker.'

He looked at the bus disappearing into the night. 'I was talking about you' he continued, quietly.

'Me?' said a nearby voice that made Hayden jump.

'What?' He looked around, that odd-looking chap was closer than he'd first realised.

'Did you call me a wanker?' the chap asked.

'What? No!' replied Hayden. 'I was talking to myself.'

'So you called yourself a wanker?' the chap asked again.

Hayden groaned. 'No, the girl on the bus.'

'I know' said the chap with what may have been a grin, behind the beard.

Hayden raised an eyebrow. 'Were you listening to our conversation?'

'I was' he replied, guiltily.

'Why?'

'I recognised the name of the fellow you were talking about.'

'Jet Tea?' asked Hayden. 'Or Rick?'

'Jet Tea.'

Hayden shrugged. Small world. Jet Tea goes out a lot. No big deal. He nodded politely at the bearded chap and started for home.

'I feel just terrible' the chap shouted back at him. Hayden stopped and turned.

'What? Why?'

'Because it's my fault.'

'What is?' Hayden was getting irate at this round-about and time-wasting conversation. The chap stepped towards him.

'It's my fault Jet Tea is acting that way towards women' he said. 'I put a spell on him.'

Hayden nodded and turned away. 'Cheers' he said as he tried to depart, only to be thwarted by a barrier of road traffic.

'Listen' shouted the chap. 'My name is Niall. I met a woman called Tara a few weeks ago who was feeling bad about dumping her boyfriend. I told her I was a wizard and she took the piss out of me, so I did a spell.'

'Wizard?'

'I did a love spell, made it out to her that it would help alleviate her guilt, because Jet Tea would instantly forget his attachment to her and fall in love with the next girl he met.'

Hayden blinked. 'That does actually explain quite a bit…'

'However' Niall continued, 'I left out the fact that the love wouldn't be reciprocated, and that it wasn't limited to the next girl, but every girl he'd communicate with thereafter.'

There was a pause. Hayden didn't know whether to laugh or run.

'Cheers' he said again. 'Jet Tea's just going through what anyone goes through after that kind of break-up.'

'Is he?' asked Niall. 'Has he mentioned Tara to you even once since it happened?'

Hayden recalled the day after the break-up; how Jet Tea said it had happened weeks ago when in fact it had only been twenty-four hours.

'No' he said. 'But that's Jet Tea, he's pretty reserved. He was the same when his-'

Niall interrupted. 'His best friends, and he doesn't mention his long term girlfriend in the wake of their break-up, not even once?'

'Has Maurice put you up to this?' asked Hayden, unsure of what kind of response to expect.

'You don't have to believe me mate' said Niall. 'I'm just trying to quell my own guilt. I'm a regular at The Good Yarn in Uxbridge. I'll be there tomorrow evening. If you give the remotest shit about your friend, tell him to come and see me.'

'Fuck off' replied Hayden. Niall shrugged and walked away.

Niall

That night Hayden lay on his bed. He couldn't sleep, he hadn't even undressed. He'd turned his phone off because it kept ringing, plus his encounter with Niall the so-called wizard had irritated him beyond peace. How could he sleep when some nutcase was gallivanting around out there, taking bizarre credit for his best friend's misery? How dare he? Had Tara put him up to it in some pointlessly nasty attempt to add insult to injury, taking dignity away from the man whose heart she'd already broken? No, Tara wasn't like that. Hayden never quite fully gleaned why she had broken up with Jet Tea, but having known her for a while now, he knew she'd never do something that bad without a very good reason.

The chance meeting with Niall had been playing on his mind for close to an hour, but drowsiness came eventually. Hayden decided that he'd tell Jet Tea about the wizard tomorrow, first thing. Even if this man was out of his mind, it was still Jet Tea's right to know of his existence. That was Hayden's last conscious thought before sleep took him.

'What?' Jet Tea sounded sterner than Hayden had ever heard him, even over the phone.

'A wizard. That's what he called himself' said Hayden.

'And you reckon he put a spell on me?'

'That's what he said. Listen mate, all I'm doing is letting you know what he said. Just remember that.'

Jet Tea sighed, his breath distorting through the phone receiver and sounding like deafening white noise to Hayden on the other end.

'He said he drinks at the Good Yarn, and that he'd be there tonight. Are you working?'

'No' said Jet Tea. 'I quit my job today.'

'Why?'

'I can't go to the Yarn' he continued, ignoring Hayden's inquiry.

'Why not?' asked Hayden.

'Because I went there last night with Maurice.'

'So?'

'We got into an argument with this guy who was harassing Gemma' he replied, altering the facts slightly. 'I called him a cunt and he turned on me.'

'What, he hit you?'

'Yeah and he said he'd break my neck next time.'

Another one, thought Hayden. His friends were being attacked left, right and center these days.

He paused for a moment. 'Even if he's there, he won't hit you again' he said reassuringly.

'How do you know?'

'Because he'd be stupid to do so. As far as he's concerned, it's a miracle you haven't reported it to the police' Hayden winced at his own words. 'So if he saw you again there's no way in hell he'd attack you, especially not in the same pub.'

Jet Tea said nothing. Hayden continued. 'Do you want to know what this wizard guy is on about or not?' he asked.

'I suppose so…'

'Right then. I'll be round yours later. I'll get Maurice to come too; we'll be in the corner for moral support.'

'You can't be with me?' asked Jet Tea, worriedly.

'No, we don't want to intimidate the guy. If he's a nutter, anything could set him off.'

'Fair enough.'

'See you soon' said Hayden. Jet Tea said nothing in reply, he simply hung up.

Several hours later, Hayden stood outside Jet Tea's bedroom door. His mum had let him in and he'd smilingly tiptoed through the front room and up the stairs with the same uncertain timidity he always adopted when invading the personal space of a friend's parent. That had never gone away since primary school. Hayden sighed.

He knocked on the door, a meagre groan from within bade him entry.

The first thing Hayden noticed was how dark it was in Jet Tea's room. The curtains were drawn and the light was off. Only the ugly blue-green glare of his oversized television prevented utter blackness. His eyes travelled from the open doorway along the floor, following an impressive trail of crusty dinner plates, crumpled fast food bags and drink-stained glasses and mugs which littered the carpet, complimented by what looked like used tissues and, although Hayden couldn't completely make it out in the twilight, a DVD case for the film *When Harry Met Sally*. Eventually his eyes fell on his friend, who was almost buried under his duvet, eyes fixed steadfastly on the television screen which reflected in his glasses. Jet Tea had not acknowledged Hayden since letting him in the room. He looked broken, dead even. He could well have breathed his last between his inviting grunt and Hayden opening the door for all he knew. For the first time since the break-up, Hayden beheld the sum of Jet Tea's recent experiences, experiences which he silently goaded himself for not taking as seriously as he should have. Everything from last night's attack right back through the tragedy of Jo 'The Hat' and Gemma's shunning to the big break-up itself were displayed on his poor friend's countenance. More than ever, Jet Tea looked like an innocent child reeling from undeserved abuse.

'You alright mate?' asked Hayden, meekly.

Jet Tea nodded difficultly, implying that had been the most movement he'd attempted since hanging up on Hayden that afternoon.

'We should head off soon' he continued. 'Maurice will be a bit late, he's just finishing some vocals.'

Jet Tea shrugged. 'Won't be long' he muttered.

Hayden scanned the environment again. 'When's the last time you tidied up?' he asked. 'It's never usually this messy.'

His friend shrugged again. 'I like it' he said. 'It looks lived in.'

'It looks died in' Hayden countered.

Jet Tea sat up slightly, stretched his arms out (Hayden was silently relieved that they were still there) and removed his duvet. He was dressed, at least. He got out of his bed and walked past an apprehensive Hayden, without offering a glance.

'Let's go' he mumbled.

They walked to the Good Yarn, through the waning daylight of the coming evening. The humble, residential aesthetic of Denham and Uxbridge, with its pleasant houses and rows of deliberately-placed trees, temporarily allowed Hayden to forget all of the horrid things he and his friends had been through in recent weeks; horrid things that were more or less their own doing, of course. He wondered. Had they been so deliriously arrogant all this time that it had completely failed to occur to either of them that their righteous indignation was undeserved? Jet Tea did call Craig a cunt, which isn't nice at all. Maurice did steal something he should have paid for. The golf club was probably a bit much, as well.

But was arrogance the right word? Were they really at all deserving of the punishments they received (and in Hayden's case, would be receiving)? He knew Jet Tea; he was rarely ever hostile without a very good reason. That Craig chap probably was being a cunt. A beating as severe as the one Maurice received is never a just punishment, let alone for the theft of a mere carrier bag. And how far would that self-important commuter have gone if Hayden hadn't subdued him? Was it hypocritical, though, to believe Maurice was undeserving of violence but this man was, just because Maurice is on Hayden's side?

'Gemma drinks there as well' said Jet Tea, cutting through Hayden's introspection, concern evident in his voice.

'I'm sorry?' Hayden replied.

'Gemma says she drinks in the Yarn now instead of the Treaty.'

'Why's that?' asked Hayden, fighting a smirk.

'Don't know.'

'So what, any way?'

Jet Tea didn't want to admit that he'd arrived at

a point in which seeing her would cause his stomach to leap into his throat. That to simply be in the same room would likely cause him to collapse in on himself as he would be forced to recall those horrific, imagined images that came to him as she and Craig slunk away into darkness to go and enjoy each other's private parts. He had a lot on his mind already with the anticipation of meeting a man he knew nothing about, save for the fact that he liked to think he possessed magical powers. That solitary facet of his personality was hardly a calming one. The possibility that Gemma might be gratuitously thrown into this scenario was too much to handle. Why couldn't Hayden have suggested to the wizard that they meet in one of the nicer, less-frequented pubs in town? The Three Tuns or the posh one where Hayden worked?

It didn't matter now; the Good Yarn was already visible on the horizon. A refuge for people that Jet Tea didn't want to see, yet despite that it was exactly where he was headed.

Hayden's phone buzzed from within his pocket as they arrived at the pub's door. He took it out and looked at it.

'It's Maurice' he said. 'He's round the corner.'

'Cool' said Jet Tea.

'I'll wait out here for him, you go on in.'

Jet Tea gasped. 'But I don't know who I'm looking for.'

'You won't miss him' said Hayden. 'He has a massive dark beard and dresses like he hasn't been indoors in years.'

'Okay' said Jet Tea, warily.

Hayden patted his friend on the shoulder affectionately. 'See you in a bit mate' he said.

With a deep breath, Jet Tea pushed open the door and stepped into the fray. He saw her instantly. His heart began racing. The worst case scenario realised. She was standing at the bar, seemingly waiting for service. He scanned the room and saw Annie, the girl Maurice had gone home with last night, alone at a table in the corner. At least Gemma hadn't brought an army with her like last time. Plus Craig didn't seem to be there, either. What now? It'd be a matter of seconds before she noticed him, and he couldn't call on his friends to save him this time, because their not being there was already part of the plan. Time to go it alone, thought Jet Tea. Without further hesitation he decided he'd walk straight up to Gemma and just make his presence known.

'Hello Gemma' he said, standing behind her.

Gemma spun round in surprise. 'Oh, Jet Tea'

she gasped.

'How's things?'

'Yeah' she said, nodding slowly. 'Not bad thanks.' She paused. 'Sorry about last night.'

'What about it?' asked Jet Tea with a shrug.

'You know, siding with that wanker who hit you. It wasn't on. I was a wee bit pissed, you know?'

A glimmer of hope came from Gemma's choice of words.

'Wanker? You mean Craig?' said Jet Tea.

'Yeah. I didn't go home with him, by the way' she replied.

'Really?'

'Yeah. I was walking with him to his bus stop and I just thought "what the fuck am I doing?" and decided to go home. He was pretty angry about it.'

Jet Tea feigned nonchalance as best he could in the face of these emerging facts. 'Fair enough. What about the other bloke?'

'What other bloke?'

'The one who gave you the book.'

'Oh him' said Gemma, bluntly. 'He's nothing. I'm not interested in him anymore. Anyway, I have to be off, having a few celebratory drinks with my friend tonight.' She turned to depart, having received her drinks.

'What are you celebrating?' asked Jet Tea.

'My new job. I'm starting work at a children's hospital in New Zealand. Just found out today.'

Jet Tea opened his mouth to speak, but found he had nothing to say.

'See you' said Gemma, with a smile; a smile that he didn't want to lose. She turned away and that smile was gone. Jet Tea immediately closed his eyes in an attempt to hold onto it in his mind. It worked for a little while, but then it faded yet again, and this time he may never get to see another one. Terrible irony. Last night and most of today, Gemma's smile was stuck in his head, it was directed at Craig and it made him feel sick. He wanted nothing more than to be rid of it, but he was burdened with it. Now, bereft of any words to keep her near to him, her smile was restored to its former glory, yet he couldn't picture it. She was now a distant, fuzzy blur in a dark corner of a rubbish pub. Soon, she'd be less than that. Jet Tea didn't know what to feel. He ordered a pint. Somehow, for the second night in a row, he was by himself in a pub he hated. This time he didn't even want to be there. He felt coerced into doing so against his will, compliant through his overly-agreeable nature. This wizard had better be a worthy conversationalist.

'Jet Tea?'

It wasn't a voice he recognised, but it was oddly familiar. Breaking out of his despairing sulk, he looked up and saw a man fitting the description Hayden had given. He looked familiar as well.

'Are you Niall?' asked Jet Tea.

'Yes' he replied solemnly. 'Shall we grab a table?'

Jet Tea bit his lip. Niall continued. 'I assume you're here to see me?'

He nodded.

'Fair enough. Let's have a seat.'

Without saying a word, Jet Tea followed Niall to an empty table. It was as far away as possible from Gemma's, which was either a good thing or a bad thing; he hadn't made up his mind. They sat down.

'So' said Niall. 'I take it your friend told you all about the curse?'

Jet Tea was nervous. He wanted to laugh condescendingly in this weirdo's face, but he couldn't anticipate a reaction. He sipped his drink calmly. 'Yes' he said.

'Okay' Niall continued. 'I'm aware this is a bit strange, and that you're clearly only here out of curiosity. You probably think I'm taking the piss.'

'That's right' said Jet Tea. 'How did you recognise me?'

'That's part of it' said Niall. 'It all started with a photograph.'

'Go on.'

Niall told him about the night he bumped into Tara, how he took the photograph of the two of them and then he began divulging details of the curse itself.

'I'd already done it before' he said. 'So I knew it would work. I was pissed off about being punished for doing it and then this bitch turns up and laughs at me, doesn't take me seriously at all.'

'Tara aint a bitch.'

'Sorry. Anyway she didn't believe a word I was saying, so I thought I'd do it. In hindsight what I should have done is something to her. Something to show her there and then that I was for real. But taking it out on someone she cared about was good enough at the time. Unfortunately, I'm not a complete wanker.'

'I'm sorry?' asked Jet Tea. He thought he saw Maurice and Hayden sit down at a distant table at the edge of his periphery.

'I started feeling bad' said Niall. 'Then I couldn't stop thinking about it. I didn't even know you, but I'd seen you. You were in here a few weeks ago with a couple of friends.'

Jet Tea tried to think of the instance Niall was referring to. Then he remembered why he recognised him. 'Gandalf?' he said.

Niall winced. 'You seemed so tiny and innocent. You look a lot younger than you are, you know. I saw you and felt even more guilty. And the icing on the cake was the conversation I overheard last night on the bus, between your friend and that girl. The gravity of what I'd done completely hit home.'

'So how does it work?' Jet Tea asked.

'You believe me?' Niall replied. 'I mean, you don't just think I'm a nutter?'

'No, no. I do think you're a nutter. I just want to hear what you have to say.'

Niall took a deep breath. 'The curse works like this' he said. 'The process is set in motion the moment your heart is broken. From that moment on the chemistry is boiling up inside you. Once you've completely let it out and come to terms with what has happened, which usually takes a few hours, it begins. The overbearing thoughts of the one who broke your heart are expelled, pushed back to somewhere deep in your subconscious.'

Jet Tea shook his head, failing to suppress a grin of disbelief.

'Tell me' said Niall. 'Have you thought about Tara much since the day she dumped you?'

He looked up. No. Not really, but what business was it of this idiot to know that? He shrugged. Niall continued.

'And did you experience a kind of stabbing pain in your chest that got worse throughout the day?'

'Yes…'

Niall sat back with triumphant resignation.

'But isn't that how heartache works?' asked Jet Tea. 'I mean, it's in the name, isn't it?'

Niall paused. Ignoring the question, he went on. 'You see, I appealed to Tara. I made out that the trick would benefit her and alleviate her guilt. I misled her.'

'How?'

'She wanted to break up with you, but couldn't bear to hurt you. I told her that through this trick you'd instantly forget her and fall in love with the next person you'd meet. She went for that.'

'So what?' said Jet Tea.

'What I deliberately neglected to mention' said Niall, 'is that you'd fall in love with every girl that paid the remotest bit of attention to you, and that the love

271

wouldn't necessarily be reciprocated. You were doomed to go through hell, but I simply told her you'd forget her.'

'I haven't fallen in love with anyone!' Jet Tea protested defiantly.

'Yeah' laughed Niall. 'That's another part of the curse; extreme denial.'

'Whatever' Jet Tea groaned. 'How does the curse work?'

'I just told you' said Niall.

'No, I mean the actual process. How do you do it?'

Niall hesitated. 'It's a love curse, Jet Tea. You really don't want to know.'

'Yes I do.'

'No, you really don't. All I'll say is that it involves the instigator of the curse having to momentarily forget all emotional bonds with the victim. Don't ask how again.'

His words, and the sincerity of their delivery, unsettled Jet Tea. He said no more on the subject.

'Fine' he said, taking a swig from his beer. 'Just tell me how to end it and I'll go.'

'So you believe me?'

'No. I don't believe you. But whatever you

reckon can break the curse, it can't hurt to try.'

Niall nodded, slowly. He leant back in his chair again.

'Bit of a problem there' he said hesitantly. 'I don't know.'

'I'm sorry?' asked Jet Tea.

'I don't know how to lift the curse' said Niall. 'Sorry.'

Jet Tea sat up. He could feel his eyes widen with anger and his nostrils flare. This man wasn't insane at all. He was taking him for a fool; sitting there laughing to himself at Jet Tea's distress, making up utter nonsense about love curses and magic and then dismissing essential details. He was so angry. How dare a complete stranger mock his situation like this? He gazed at Niall opposite him; he looked so blasé, so indifferent to everything. It was now ridiculously clear that he was only there to laugh in his face. Shame on Hayden for buying into it; he was somewhat to blame for all of this as well. Jet Tea could feel his fingers trying violently to sink into the wooden table beneath them. His teeth began to grind. The walls looked as though they were peeling away around him. His chair wobbled. He wanted to explode.

So he did.

Reality Steps Aside

It was a coloured space, multicoloured. However, there were no definitions to the multitude of colours. Wherever Jet Tea looked, he saw a different colour, but he could not define where one ended and a new began. They weren't segmented like patchwork or gradually changing like an old computer's screen-saver, nor were they of a gradient and blending into one another. By all rights, there should really have only been one surrounding colour, but Jet Tea's sensory perception insisted there were many.

To make matters worse, the colourful surrounding wasn't giving off the appropriate vibe that would lead Jet Tea to believe he was in a room; he could not judge the distance of what was in front of him. They could have been inches from his nose, or they could have been several miles in the distance. Like fog, no matter how far into it Jet Tea moved, the atmosphere always appeared ahead of him, with no hint at getting any closer.

The ground, or rather what should have been the ground, was no different. Jet Tea felt that he was standing on something, but the lack of definition to the surrounding dimensions made him too apprehensive to relax, but too baffled to panic.

'What's happened?' he shouted. There seemed to be nothing to shout at in sight, but it couldn't have hurt to try.

Resigning himself to the likelihood that he wouldn't be answered, Jet Tea decided to explore, if an unrefined void with no physical features and contours can even be explored. His first instinct was to find out if movement wasn't limited by gravity and obstacle, like in the environment he should have been in. So he began to walk, stepping enthusiastically in a downward motion as though he were descending a flight of stairs. To what would have been his amazement, had he enjoyed being in this place, Jet Tea found himself moving steadily downwards through the space he inhabited. The object-less view around him didn't allow it to look like he was moving at all, let alone in an extraordinary direction, but he knew he was. He felt like he was, it was a sensation akin to that of lying or sitting perfectly still for a certain amount of time until you feel as though you are moving at incredible speed.

Jet Tea continued to explore the space in the most creative ways he could think of. Eventually, after learning he could walk in any direction he wanted to, including diagonally upwards and downwards, he grew tired of simply walking. His next desire was to move without any manipulation of his limbs. He achieved this with surprising ease; he only had to imagine the direction in which he wished to be going and he found himself gliding gracefully in that direction. This managed to bring the elusive smile to Jet Tea's face as he floated, arms waving theatrically, about the place.

Having perfected thought-controlled movement, and becoming so engrossed in this new-found ability that he almost forgot he was in a perpetual nothing with no means of escape, Jet Tea began slowly rolling, spinning and tumbling every which way. Were anybody else present he would have looked like one of those modern circus performers who manage to perform elegant ballet at terrifying heights while suspended on wires. His long hair waved and fell accordingly, which allowed him to remain aware of when he was upside-down and when he was positioned correctly.

Jet Tea's blissful floating throughout the colourful void was abruptly disrupted by what felt like a shudder, as though a pulse had been sent through the space he inhabited.

He rotated to an upstanding position.

'Who's that?' he said.

A voice, that seemed to come from nowhere but was simultaneously all around him, boomed its reply.

'Jet Tea' it said.

'Yeah' Jet Tea replied. 'What?'

'Hi' it said. Jet Tea felt the conversation would be annoyingly round-about.

'Hello' he said.

'How's it going?'

Jet Tea took a deep, agitated breath. 'I'm alright mate' he said. 'What's happening here then?'

A wooden chair tumbled at alarming speed toward him. It hit his knee and ricocheted off to one side. He grabbed his knee in pain and uttered an unintentionally high-pitched squeal as the chair came apart like a vegetable stock cube hitting hot water, until eventually no traces were visible.

'Blimey' he said. 'What's that all about?' A

fork and a small hardback book appeared and behaved similarly, both fortunately missing him this time.

The voice spoke again. 'Reality is at odds with itself' it said.

'What?' said Jet Tea.

'I've pulled reality apart for a moment' the voice continued, 'so I can appropriately explain what's going on.' Jet Tea was lost. 'The chairs and things are reality trying to force itself back together and be manifest again. But this is nicer, isn't it?'

'It's alright' replied Jet Tea, 'I like the flying and that.'

'Yes I saw you enjoyed flying about. Good for you' said Jet Tea's invisible new friend. 'You know, in this reality you have every power imaginable.'

'What?'

'You can do anything' said the voice. 'While you are here you have limitless power.'

Jet Tea's mouth hung open for several seconds. 'How?'

'You are magic. Or you will be. This reality *is you*. You just have to work out how to do it, which will likely take longer than you've got.'

He grabbed his chin in thought. 'Could I,' Jet Tea said, 'create a rock so heavy that no one can move it?'

'Why, yes' boomed the voice. 'The concept of limitless power has no boundaries.'

Jet Tea spied an opportunity to annoy someone. 'Even me?'

'Indeed.'

'But then if I can't move it, that means I can't do everything, doesn't it?'

There was a silence.

'The concept of limitless power-' the voice stopped. 'Don't make a rock.'

'Hang on-' Jet Tea began, suddenly remembering the moving fluorescent light in the pub toilet, the bottle that slid across the table and everything that came after. 'Is that what all that weird shit was about?'

'Weird shit?' it asked in response.

'Like loads of stuff was moving, like in a ghost film' he sort-of explained.

The voice replied, in a newfound enlightened tone. 'Ah' it said 'that would have happened ever since you became infected.'

Jet Tea cocked his head at an angle in confusion.

'As soon as you were touched by magic, you

were venturing toward a point where reality would step aside for you. The things you've been seeing' it paused, 'were the first traces of that.'

'But where am I?' Jet Tea asked.

'Like I said, you're in a space outside reality' replied the being. 'Well, your reality. This is my reality. I maintain its existence by thinking about it. I think, therefore we are.'

'But you said this place *was* me, or something.'

'It is, but someone still needs to look after it.'

'Why?'

'That spell put on you' it continued.

Jet Tea huffed. 'Yeah, I heard about that.'

'All the magic converging on you, and the confusion, it was only a matter of time before you'd be dragged out of reality.' Jet Tea looked alarmed as the prospect of never returning dawned on him. His first thought was of a recently-used dinner plate resting on a pillow. That was his immediate image of reality.

'Don't worry' the thing continued. 'You'll be back in a little bit.'

It had a friendly, if ominously deep, tone of voice. Speaking to it was like being told stories as a child by a grandparent. He wanted to get back to the status quo as soon as possible, but for the time being Jet

281

Tea was happy to talk.

'I don't get all the words you're saying' said Jet Tea. 'Manu-fest reality? What?'

'Manifest' the being corrected him. 'Your reality is a very tough place, full of cement and stars and clouds and heavy things to stop it from ceasing to exist. It's doing all it can to pull itself back together and in a short time it will.'

'What will happen to you?' Jet Tea asked. 'And who are you?'

The being answered his two questions in reverse order. 'I am Niall, and I will still be here. There will simply be fewer flying chairs when you're gone.'

'Niall the wizard?' Jet Tea gasped. Then the dusty explosion that happened to the chair, the fork and the book happened again, but in reverse. Then, the face of Niall the wizard, albeit bigger, stretched wider and with its edges somehow blending into the surrounding colour, bubbled into view above Jet Tea, smiling.

'Oh blimey' said Jet Tea, taken aback but glad that there were still things that could surprise him.

'Hello' Niall said again.

'Right then' laughed Jet Tea, nervously. He squinted at Niall's face as his glasses slid down his nose slightly. 'Hang about' he continued. 'How are you always here? I saw the proper you a minute ago.'

'You did indeed' said Niall, maintaining his happy-to-explain tone. 'I am not the proper me. I am an isolated consciousness.'

Jet Tea stared blankly, feeling that begging his pardon would be a redundant venture. Niall spoke more. 'The Niall you know was constantly irritated by his ability to harness magic. Almost always in pain and being distracted from-' the face glided to one side and back again as a television remote control hurtled past and disintegrated. '-Being distracted from everything.'

Jet Tea nodded slowly, implying that he was just about up to speed with what Niall was explaining to him.

'He found a way to isolate the section of his consciousness that can control magic, because that was the section that was, as you've probably gathered, causing the pain.'

Jet Tea had not gathered. He was too overwhelmed by everything to properly pay attention.

Niall sighed. 'The real-world Niall can still access my magical powers, but he now no longer has the burden of an over-active consciousness rattling away inside his modest human brain. He can get on with life comfortably while I exist in a separate dimension from my corporeal form. This dimension.'

A moment's silence passed and Jet Tea wriggled and screwed up his face in frustration. 'Corporate what?' he hissed angrily. 'Can I go now?' Niall's face twisted into a broad smile.

'Why am I cursed?' Jet Tea cried. 'It's not fair. What the fuck have I done to get a magic spell thing going on?'

The reply disappointed him. 'Jet Tea' said Niall. 'You have done nothing, you know this.'

'So why all the hassle?' he appealed.

'Bad things happen to everybody, Jet Tea' the face boomed.

'And since when was all this crazy nonsense real?' Jet Tea asked.

Niall laughed softly - or at least a giant magical spirit face's best attempt at softly. 'Magic has been real for a while now' he said. 'It's not worth going into.'

'So can I get superpowers or something?'

'That would be silly, wouldn't it?' said Niall. Jet Tea floated smoothly through the rainbow-void and set down next to the giant head.

'I suppose' he sighed. 'Is there a way to-' he was interrupted by another shuddering pulse, and to his left he saw a brown streak fade into view. A crashing sound to his right caused him to swing his head in that direction, in time to see a wooden table spinning toward him. Jet Tea looked all around, the brown streak was now surrounding him, and had become defined enough for him to realise it was a skirting board, with the cream-coloured walls of the pub gradually stretching out from it.

The relative earth-quake of activity around him did not stop him from asking his question. 'Can I stop the curse?' he asked. 'I don't like it.'

'You can' said Niall, who then opted to laugh as opposed to actually help.

'Please' said Jet Tea as a cardboard wine list dropped from above. 'You're still human aren't you? I mean, you didn't come from nothing, did you?' Jet Tea felt his eyes moisten, and his vision momentarily blurred until the first few tears were blinked from it. 'Give us a hand mate' he cried.

Niall flashed the frown of a caricature. 'Poor Jet Tea' he said. 'There is a way.'

'Yeah?' replied Jet Tea with some hope.

'It's not exactly straightforward, though.'

Jet Tea lowered his head through disappointment. He was momentarily knocked off balance by a flourishing cluster of laminate floor tiles, but managed to right himself. 'What is it then?' he asked.

'I-' Niall spoke no more. The atmosphere rumbled and shook, as the lumber of the pub walls and ceiling piled in around Jet Tea, blocking Niall's face from sight. Inanimate objects, in this case very much animate, swirled and poured into existence, shaking Jet Tea to the ground and closing the magical void shut. He cried out in vain protest as the room began to take shape and the last traces of brilliant colour vanished behind the pale walls of reality.

Silence.

His eyes opened. Jet Tea found himself in a crumpled heap; face down on the hard pub floor. It took a few moments for his senses to gather together, but when they did, he looked up.

'Niall!' he gasped. 'Did you hypnotise me? No, you spiked my drink!' Niall sat at the table, as before, staring confusedly at the fallen Jet Tea, who sat up and pushed his drink away warily.

'Are you alright?' he asked. 'You fell off your chair.'

Jet Tea said nothing. He looked around. Gemma's table was unoccupied, save for two empty glasses. She'd disappeared, most likely forever, and he hadn't even noticed her leave. What would have been joy at being back in the real world was instead anger at not having retrieved an answer to his question. He sprang to his feet, causing Niall to shift back in his chair to avoid him. Then he ran over to the opposite wall and stopped, facing it.

Niall called over, but Jet Tea continued to ignore him. Instead he raised his little arms in the air and pounded the wall in frustration, screaming. This persisted for several seconds before Jet Tea gave in to defeat and staggered sullenly back to his chair. For a while, all there was to fill the time was awkward non-conversation. In Niall's defence, it's never easy to find the right thing to say when someone you've just met falls off of a chair and promptly decides to beat up a wall. Silence is the only sensible course of action in such a scenario.

Jet Tea broke it. 'Can I go back?'

'Go back?' Niall asked and echoed.

'Yeah.'

'I don't know.'

Silence resumed, with Jet Tea staring solemnly toward the ground. Eventually Niall, who despite his resignation from the conversation did not know where

Jet Tea was talking about, allowed his curiosity to take charge. 'Go back where?' he asked.

'To the place' Jet Tea said, unsure of how to describe the place. 'The colourful flying place.'

Niall raised his eyebrows. 'Oh,' he said. 'You went *there.*'

'What did you think I was talking about?' asked Jet Tea.

'I don't know, I just thought you were talking bollocks' the magician abruptly replied. 'You just fell off a chair and beat up a wall. I didn't think there was any point in asking you what you were going on about.'

Jet Tea nodded in admittance. 'How come you don't know?' he asked. 'You were in there.'

Niall sighed. 'Nobody ever gets it' he muttered. 'Even though it's explained.' He reluctantly continued. 'The version of me you met in the void is a separate part of my consciousness that I managed to isolate because it was giving me headaches. I don't actually access it.'

Jet Tea nodded, without removing his gaze. 'Oh yeah, he did say.'

'I should ask' said Niall. 'How is he?'

'The other you?' Jet Tea asked in reply

'Yeah. Is he angry? Locked away in a void between realities and that, can't be good.'

'He didn't seem all that bothered.'

'That's good.' Niall sat up. 'Why do you want to go back?' he asked.

'Because,' Jet Tea took a long, deep breath to try and relieve his frustration. 'I asked a question and he never got round to answering it.'

Niall bit his lip. Having put the curse on Jet Tea in the first place, he felt somewhat responsible for the man's misery. 'What do you need to know?'

Jet Tea opened his mouth to reply, but paused. 'I asked-' he paused again. For some reason, recalling his question made him feel a bit dizzy and light-headed. He spoke again. 'I asked if there was-'

The reason for the sudden dizziness quickly dawned on Jet Tea. He noisily slid his chair backwards and shot to his feet, startling Niall.

'I know!' Jet Tea cried optimistically. 'He did answer!'

As it so happened, the magical version of Niall did get round to answering Jet Tea's question, but as Jet Tea was halfway back to his reality when he did so, the answer only got as far as his subconscious; lying in wait to spring to mind the moment Jet Tea thought about the question.

Niall was visibly relieved at Jet Tea's sudden

elation, but was also utterly baffled. 'What is it?' he asked, catching some of Jet Tea's excitement in his voice. Jet Tea did not reply. Instead he lunged toward Niall with a grin that stretched across his whole face and giggled excitedly, jabbing the magician rapidly in the arm with his two index fingers. He recoiled, wiggling his fingers with ecstasy and then darted out of the room, still giggling.

Niall shook his head, smiling. He assumed the fading of Jet Tea's giggle meant that he was now too far away to be heard, but was proven wrong by one faint cry of 'I know!'

A Reflection on Events

Maurice and Hayden watched with fond smiles as Jet Tea bounced and skipped optimistically from the pub, screaming 'I know!' They'd entered shortly before, missing Gemma and Annie by seconds.

'Wonder what that was about?' asked Maurice.

'Jet Tea has been acting really strange for a while now' Hayden replied.

'Well that's obviously because of Tara, isn't it?'

'Is it?' asked Hayden. 'I don't know. He hasn't mentioned her at all since they broke up.'

Maurice thought for a moment. 'There are thousands of ways to deal with a break-up' he said. 'Do you think that just because he hasn't mentioned her she hasn't been on his mind?'

'All of his negativity over the last few weeks seemed to be over that Scottish girl, Gemma' said Hayden.

'Rebounds, Jet Tea said' replied Maurice. 'He was talking bollocks about her being in love with him, or something, but he was really talking about himself. He's feeling worse than anyone usually would about a girl they barely know, because of Tara. Think about it; he's only spoken to her two or three times, yet he's constantly texting her. Did he mention that he personally delivered his copy of *1984* to her flat?'

'How did he find out where she lives?'

'Who knows? But my point is he wouldn't be behaving this way towards her other than in the wake of being dumped.'

Hayden sighed. 'Do you want another pint?' he asked.

'Yes please' replied Maurice.

Whilst waiting for their beers to be poured, Hayden wondered whether he should tell Maurice about the wizard. Since their meeting at the bus stop he'd began to relax his aggressive skepticism about the whole thing. Jet Tea had never behaved like this before, and Tara ending their relationship was not the worst thing that had ever happened to him. There were violent waves of extreme happiness and excitement followed swiftly by long periods of immovable despair and a deep introspectiveness that he'd never seen in his friend before.

As the pints were delivered and money was exchanged, Hayden looked over at Maurice. He was wearing his glasses, which he rarely did, and sat in what looked like deep thought as he stared into space. So often had he laughingly beheld Maurice, pissed out of his skull and shrieking maniacally at the ceiling of some unfamiliar, hostile pub while irate bar staff pleaded with him to get off the table and put his trousers back on that it was easy to forget about the intense, amazing brain that lay buried under the pulp of alcohol-abuse and blithering, self-made carnage. Hayden enjoyed nights like this. When the time came that they'd each go their separate ways for whatever reason and evenings in each other's company would be few and far between he was sure that it would be these nights; the tame, reflective, quiet ones that he'd remember most fondly. As fun as it was to make short work of eight cans of lager before jumping on a bus in the pouring rain to the other side of London and spend the night in a sweaty corner shouting abuse at overly serious open-mic performers, there was only ever emptiness and shame that followed. Nights that he could take something away from and retain long after the hangover had passed, they were the special ones.

'I wonder where Jet Tea went?' said Maurice, as Hayden returned.

'Maurice' he replied. 'I should probably tell you something.'

'Go on then.'

Hayden hesitated, but continued. 'That bloke Jet Tea was talking to, he says he's a wizard.'

Maurice cocked his head in confusion. Hayden went on.

'He told me that he'd put a spell on Jet Tea, that made him fall in love with every girl he encountered, and that the spell would push Tara out of his mind completely. That's why we came here instead of the Three Tuns tonight, because it's his local.'

There was a pause before Maurice spoke. 'He's not having you on?'

'It's possible' said Hayden. 'But I thought it wouldn't hurt if Jet Tea were to meet the guy.'

'So you think it could be true?'

'I don't know.' Something about the existence of magic had recently begun to appeal to Hayden. His phone rang. He hung up instantly.

'I think' said Maurice, 'that even if it were true, this is just a magical version of exactly what Jet Tea would be going through anyway. It really makes no difference.'

'No difference at all?' asked Hayden.

'None at all. Right, he breaks up with his long-term girlfriend, instantly pretends he doesn't care and stops talking about her, then falls head-over-heels in love with the very next girl that so much as looks at him, and every subsequent woman he comes across. That isn't strange behaviour, Hayden. Although I suppose you'd have to break up with someone yourself to actually realise that.'

'I've broken up with people!' Hayden protested.

'So how does the magician fit in to all this?'

'Wizard' said Maurice.

'That's what I meant. Explain him.'

Maurice opened his mouth to speak, but paused.

'He...' he paused again. 'He's probably just some clever bastard making the most of Jet Tea's misery in order to fool people. It's working, apparently.'

Hayden nodded. 'He did say that Tara told him about Jet Tea first. Fair point.'

'We could always go and ask him what he's playing at' said Maurice. 'I'd like to know what he thinks he's gaining from all of this.'

They each looked over to his table. Niall had gone. 'Or not' Hayden replied.

'Either way' said Maurice, 'He's obviously given Jet Tea some really good news. Did you see the way he darted out?'

Hayden laughed. 'Yeah, he looks like he's back on form. Maybe we should phone him.'

'Give him time' said Maurice. 'I think things are going to change with Jet Tea now. Once he's really over this whole thing.'

'What do you mean?' asked Hayden.

'I just think change is due. Jet Tea has been stagnating in this town for a while now. We all have.'

A police siren sounded from outside the pub. Hayden almost shot up out of his seat and gasped. Then it faded.

'Are you alright?' asked Maurice.

'Change can be bad' replied Hayden, seemingly ignoring the question. His heart was pounding, but gradually returning to normal.

'So what will you be doing?' he asked.

'I reckon I might move to a different city' said Maurice. 'Maybe Berlin.'

A fleeting sense of dread passed through

Hayden.

'Really?'

'Yeah, I just think I've exhausted London.' He recalled his dream, the one in which he strolled through a dying Soho. He couldn't shake the feeling that he'd done all that damage himself and that the dream was an omen.

'It's time to move on. Also I have a sneaking suspicion that I might find love there. How about you?'

Hayden shrugged. Even this discussion about change was enough to ensure that things would never be the same again. How long can three friends in their mid-to-late twenties just saunter away their time in the local pub and each others' living rooms without thinking about what happens next? Now they were talking about it ending. Once the seeds of ambition have been sown, once the prospect begins to be entertained, change will inevitably come. That consciousness of imminent necessity can never be killed. But what would he do? Where would he go? The only two people who seemed to be able to tolerate him were on the verge of leaving and then what? Go back to work? Wake up the next day and go again, and again, and again, enduring a sea of subdued skeptics who shared nothing in common with him? There was only blackness in his version of the future. Only one place to go…

'I don't think I have much say in the matter, to be honest' he said. 'That incident on the train the other night is likely to come back to me sooner or later.'

'Do you reckon?' Maurice asked, doubtfully.

'I've had about twenty missed calls from an unknown number' said Hayden. 'The only people who phone me are you, Jet Tea and my parents. Whoever it is will eventually get bored of being hung up on and come and find me.'

'Shit, really?'

'It's that or the impending prison of sensible adulthood' laughed Hayden. 'If you two won't be around, they can do their worst.'

He sipped his beer. Maurice leant over and rubbed his friend on the shoulder, not knowing what to say.

Hayden broke the silence. 'What do you reckon Jet Tea is up to?'

'I don't know' said Maurice. 'It would have helped if that cunt wizard didn't fuck off though.'

'So you're agreeing he's a wizard now?' laughed Hayden.

'I think that if he wants to be a wizard, then who are we to tell him he isn't? If he lives in a reality where he has magical powers and can cast spells on people to make them behave in a way they were going to anyway, then he's right. It's his reality and even if we don't live in it, that doesn't make it any less a reality than ours.'

'And if he's just having us on?'

'Then he's a cunt.'

Hayden laughed, and changed the subject. 'How are you feeling lately?'

'I'm sorry?'

'Since the attack' he continued.

'Ah, right' said Maurice. 'The pain didn't last very long, really. But I've been thinking a lot about the way I was treated; by both of them. I'm getting really disillusioned with the place I grew up in.'

Hayden wasn't. The place he grew up in still contained his best friends, but once they slipped away he was certain disillusionment would arrive swiftly.

'You reckon that sort of thing wouldn't happen in Berlin?' he asked skeptically.

'I'm not saying it wouldn't' Maurice replied. 'But the different mentality over there might change me a little bit. Maybe over there I wouldn't have been so frustrated with my music, wouldn't have needed that long walk. I may not have been awake at nine in the morning. My friend tells me the nightlife over there doesn't really kick off until gone midnight. I've been considering all these factors for ages. It's time to go.'

'I should go' said Hayden.

'Really? Where are you thinking of going?'

'No, no' he continued. 'I mean go home. I'm pretty tired.'

They stood outside the pub and hugged goodbye. Just as their embrace loosened, a siren sounded yet again. Hayden nearly jumped out of his skin and behind them a blue, flashing light loomed and silhouetted the two friends ominously against their dreary surroundings. The police car was slowing.

'Shit' Hayden gasped.

'What?' asked Maurice.

'How have they found me?'

Hayden had a look of terror in his widening eyes. This was it. Maurice took a deep breath as it suddenly occurred to him why his friend had become so frantic. Hayden looked at the approaching vehicle; it wasn't extremely close, just yet. Thankfully he knew Uxbridge's alleys and backstreets as well as anyone. There was still a way out, but he'd have to be quick. He strode backwards.

'I have to go' he said to Maurice. Then, spying

his exit in the form of a dark alley that ran alongside the pub they'd just left, hopped into a sprint and faded into shadow.

The Triumph of Jet Tea

Jet Tea clenched his steering wheel tightly as he hurtled down the duel carriageway, *Debaser* by the Pixies flooding his small car and drowning out any other possible noise. Since receiving the answer to his question (which, in hindsight, was now painfully obvious) he'd sprinted home, made short work of a mug of tea and pulled his Pixies t-shirt from the wash basket before changing into it. He then darted back out and hopped into his car.

He was fast on the way to the final stage of his unfortunate trial. It hadn't occurred to him once during recent weeks, but now he chuckled to himself at his gigantic oversight. All of those women; Gemma, Jo 'The Hat', Jessica, Alice and countless others who'd crossed his path only momentarily. Through all of them, he'd failed to consider that there was one woman out there who could obviously solve all of his problems; Tara.

Whether or not Niall was genuine or fraudulent had become irrelevant now. He certainly wasn't wrong in pointing out that Jet Tea hadn't thought about his ex once since she ended their relationship. How did that fact fail to ring alarm bells? Jet Tea hadn't been in enough relationships to be considered an expert on how to deal with break-ups, but he was sure that it was reasonably common to actually spend time thinking about the other person once they'd ended it. He tried to recall, but beyond his bizarre incident on the toilet several weeks ago he failed to remember a single moment spent with Tara on his mind. Until now, of course.

Then there was that other place; the magical flying place wherein the giant, disembodied head of Niall resided. Jet Tea had asked how to lift the curse, but didn't manage to get an answer. Except he did. He didn't know the answer, exactly, but he knew that he knew it. Or something. All that mattered was that he get to Tara's flat as soon as possible. That was essential. He'd work out precisely why later.

There it stood.   Unremarkable as it would appear to an impartial passer-by, the façade of Tara's building loomed overwhelmingly above Jet Tea, who felt tiny but defiant.   Her door seemed like that of a fantastical palace, with he the reluctant but bold hero who'd finally fumbled his way to the denouement of his quest despite the aggressive efforts of incidental foes along the way.   Strange, that.

A dull, yellow light shone from the window above the door.   Her window.   She was in.   Something took hold of Jet Tea and, without any apprehension or forethought whatsoever, he stepped up and rang the buzzer to her flat.   None of the self-conscious trepidation that had been prevalent when initiating conversations with Gemma or Jo 'The Hat' was there any more.   He felt completely at ease, like what he was doing was the most natural thing in the world.   How long had it been since he'd seen his ex?   Weeks?   Months?   Time hadn't really been on his mind lately.

A muffled noise clicked into being.   Tara's voice followed it through the speaker grate.

'Hello?'

'It's Jet Tea.'

She said nothing else.   The buzz sounded and Jet Tea pushed the door open, went inside and made his way upstairs.

Tara did not wait for him to knock; there she stood in the open doorway to her flat; arms folded, legs crossed, her worried eyes following him up the stairs. He arrived before her, and for several seconds nothing was said. Tara looked older than he remembered, but no less beautiful. She had a slightly unsettling countenance, one that Jet Tea had not seen upon her in the one-and-a-quarter years they'd been together. Was she worried or angry? Perhaps their imminent conversation would answer that.

'Come in' she said, flatly. Jet Tea smiled, nodded and obeyed.

They were in the corridor now; she had closed the door behind them but remained still in her spot -save for turning around- as he made his way past her.

'It's been a while' she said. 'What can I do for you?'

Suddenly, despite his previous bravado, Jet Tea found he didn't know what to say or do. He was so courageous in entering her flat that he hadn't thought any further ahead. A wave of confliction hit him; he knew Tara so well, had shared everything with her in the past and was so at ease in her company that her being there forever was his only conceivable version of reality.

But that was before. In the weeks since he'd last seen her she'd broken his heart, swiftly exited his conscious mind and bestowed upon him a pile of wonderful women who had each made a point of not being interested in him. Jet Tea's more recent problems had seen his life with Tara pale in comparison, but here she was again; and her beauty was beaming at him through an admirably defiant but vain attempt at masking it. She didn't seem like she wanted to see him (which, if he thought about it, put her on the same page as all the other women he'd met recently), but this was his Tara nonetheless. No amount of resistance or austerity on her part could change that. He gazed upon her; from her deep, dark eyes to her long, soft brown hair and down her slender body. He could see every inch of her through what she was wearing, his hands -almost involuntarily- stretched out in front of him with a striking desire to touch her once more and a firm assertiveness came upon and overwhelmed him as the very answer to his aching question achieved fruition to the last word. He knew exactly what to do.

'I need to have sex with you right now!' he exclaimed, lunging toward her.

Horrified, Tara shot back against the door. She watched momentarily as Jet Tea, with a grin that -given

307

the situation- somehow upheld his inherent innocence, made his move. He almost fell into her but she ducked swiftly beneath one of his approaching arms, escaping down the hallway and into the living room.

'What the fuck are you doing?' she screamed.

Jet Tea, confused, stumbled around to face her. She was an object that he wanted; her terrified, contorted face and posture hadn't immediately registered. As such, his approach recommenced.

'Jet Tea!' she cried. 'No!'

He stopped in his tracks, pulling his mind out of the haze she'd put it in and finally coming to realise.

Oh Christ, no. The unthinkable flashed through his mind. That wasn't who he was. He was never going to attempt *that*. His horror was now turned toward the notion that that was Tara's assumption. Never in a million years. He was just being enthusiastic, and tactless. She'd likely crush his bony frame in such a situation anyway.

'Tara!' he muttered. 'No, no!'

'Don't come near me!' she replied, edging into the furthest possible corner.

'No' he continued to protest. 'You don't understand!'

'I'm sorry?' said Tara, unapologetically. 'I

don't think you could have made it much clearer!'

'Please, listen.'

Tara shook her head. 'Get out of here' she said. 'Now!'

Jet Tea became a little boy again. His energy, his newfound superpowers, had withered away. It was unbearable to see the love of his former life look at him in this way; like he was a monster who'd invaded her home. There was no simile, he was exactly that.

'I wasn't going to try and-' he couldn't finish the sentence. The very thought of it disgusted him to his meagre bones. Nor could he fathom leaving without getting what he came for, just to go back and relive those horrid weeks again and again until he died of heartbreak or stress, or another Craig.

The firmness that led him had gone flaccid. Embarrassment arrived fashionably late to his despairing cocktail party. He felt his hands begin to shake, his eyes grow hot in their sockets. Then he gave in and burst into tears.

He didn't hold back like he did with Maurice on the night he'd been dumped, or when Hayden had entered his bedroom earlier that day. His emotion flooded from him like it should have done so many times. He broke down and bawled loudly, open mouthed and wailing like a wounded beast. Tara's look of horror changed into one of sickened pity. With trepidation, she began to approach.

Embarrassed beyond coherent words, Jet Tea flung his quivering hands over his face and cowered from Tara as she drew closer. He couldn't stop moaning through the tears, but he tried his best. There was a slither of pride left behind somewhere and he'd be cold in the ground before she'd take that away.

He felt her hand press softly on his back. It was a touch so familiar to him, and it managed to tell him that she'd forgiven his disturbing sexual outburst, for now at least. Tara had caused Jet Tea a lot of pain, but there was no way on Earth she'd ever shy away from the opportunity to comfort him in a moment of despair.

'Come and sit down with me' she said, softly rubbing his back.

He sniffed. 'Okay.'

He stood up straight and crept behind her into the living room. They collapsed onto her sofa. Through his teary eyes Jet Tea scanned the room, glancing at the kitchenette. She'd recently made dinner.

'You know' he sniveled, 'you shouldn't use a metal spatula on a non-stick frying pan. It destroys the coating.'

Tara snorted a chuckle in reply. A would-be silence followed, were it not for Jet Tea's soft weeping.

'We need to talk about that' said Tara.

'About what?'

'What do you think?' she continued.

Jet Tea looked up, adopting an expression of concern.

'I'm not a-' he started. 'I wasn't going to-'

'I know' she replied, sparing him. 'There's still a problem, though, isn't there?'

'Yes' Jet Tea replied, nodding.

'I'm sorry' said Tara. 'That's all I can say.'

'Not a single word in all this time?' said Jet Tea.

'I know. I should have been to see you in person, or at least given you a proper reason. I just thought you were thinking the same.'

'What?'

'You know' Tara continued. 'We were always arguing, your friends hated my friends, plus it was hardly going to last much longer, was it? I'm a lot older than you and we want different things.'

Jet Tea frowned. 'What are you talking about?' he said. 'I gathered all that; that was obvious. I mean you never bothered to mention the wizard.'

'Oh God.'

Niall. Jet Tea had found out about Niall. This was the last person Tara wanted to think about. She'd been so stupid in her grief, so susceptible. The disgust she held for herself hadn't worn off yet.

'Why didn't you tell me?' he asked. 'All this time!'

'You don't believe him, do you?' scoffed Tara. 'Seriously?'

'Does it matter?' said Jet Tea. 'You still did it.'

He knew about that as well?

'Did what?'

'The spell thing. The curse.'

'Oh' said Tara. 'I'm sorry about that, I was in a weird place that night; I know how ridiculous it seems now, just forget about it.'

Jet Tea sat up. 'But it isn't ridiculous' he groaned, wiping his nose with his sleeve.

'What?'

He opened his mouth to tell her about the colourful world of magic he travelled to when he'd fallen off of his chair. His ability to fly and somersault, Niall's disembodied, magical giant head. Then he thought better of it and closed his mouth.

'Never mind.'

Tara shrugged. 'How did you bump into Niall?'

312

she asked.

Jet Tea told her everything of consequence that had happened in his life since she had bowed out of it, although he told her in reverse. Meeting Niall, because he'd overheard Hayden talking to Alice on the bus; his rudeness to Alice because he'd been drowning his sorrows after being punched in the face; watching Gemma cozy up to Craig; Telling Jo 'The Hat' to fuck off; meeting her; meeting Gemma…

Tara was rather confused at his chosen structure, but she comprehended.

'Do you want a glass of wine?' she asked.

Jet Tea fought off a wince. Wine. He really didn't like it, but he'd have to this time. Why had he never gotten around to mentioning that when they were together? A little more foresight and she'd be offering him a nice cold beer right now.

'Yeah, alright' he said.

She got up and walked over to the kitchenette, pulled two wine glasses and a bottle of cheap red from the overhead cupboard and poured one.

'Or a beer?'

'Nah, wine's fine' said Jet Tea.

Tara smiled, poured a second glass and brought

them over to the sofa. She took a long, slow sip and looked at him.

'Enough is enough' she said, changing tone. 'Why did you come all the way over here to try it on with me?'

'You have to understand-' replied Jet Tea.

Tara interrupted. 'You can't have expected it to work. Really, I thought there was nothing left you could do to surprise me. But lo and behold-'

'It isn't like that' he said. 'Please just listen.'

Tara huffed. 'Go on then.'

'You're going to have to bear with me.'

'I'm more than used to your ravings by now, thank you very much' she said.

'When I met Niall earlier, I asked him how I could break the curse.'

'Oh not that fucking curse again' Tara groaned.

'Wait' said Jet Tea. 'He told me he didn't know, but shortly after that I exploded and woke up in a magical world.'

Tara's jaw dropped, slightly. Jet Tea went on.

'I could fly and everything. I asked Niall's big smiley head if *he* knew how to do it, and he was about to tell me…'

Her head drooped forward, a bit.

'But then the pub I was in blew up around me and it was too late. But it actually wasn't. The answer reached the back of my mind, and I knew it but didn't really know it-'

'Slow down, please.'

'-Until I got here.'

'And what, pray tell, does this have to do with you trying to run me over with your erection?' asked Tara.

'That's just it!' Jet Tea cried, excitedly. 'The answer was; "*the love that imprisoned you shall unbound you*", or something.'

Tara raised an eyebrow. 'I see what you're getting at' she sighed.

Jet Tea's moment of despair had mostly subsided and he felt like a man again. He looked at Tara, coiled beautifully on the edge of the sofa, clutching her glass of deep-red wine, her hair ever-so-slightly disheveled from the commotion of a few minutes before. He wanted her once again, but trial and error had allowed him to restrain himself. That was no way to behave. He sipped his wine with caution, not allowing his distaste for it to show on his face.

'Basically' he said, 'to end the curse we have to have sex one more time.'

Tara laughed dismissively. 'Yes, I knew you were going to say that.'

'It's true' said Jet Tea. 'I worked it out all by myself!'

'Well thank you' said Tara, unthankfully. 'But telling stories about giant heads and flying through magical pubs or whatever isn't a particularly great seduction technique. It's not going to happen.'

Jet Tea frowned. Tara had always been so level headed, perfectly offsetting him in his more childish moments. And now she seemed older; not just a few weeks older like she obviously was, but quite a bit older; thus wiser. The way she'd spoken to him that evening was like an enjoyable, insightful lesson at school (something he'd been bereft of). It couldn't have been possible that she was wrong this time, he'd even pondered it himself in the pub; Niall had drugged his drink, that was all. It was a hallucination that fed off of his basic desires. Of course he wanted to have sex with Tara again. To go from regular intercourse with one woman to a sudden, involuntary dry spell would doubtlessly encourage that desire. No curse was necessary there.

'I'm sorry Tara' he said amicably.

'Don't worry' she replied. 'Just don't do it

again.'

They talked and drank for a couple of hours. Jet Tea felt like he'd compiled a backlog of important things he needed to tell her about. Although it hadn't crossed his mind, he now realised that for the last few weeks he didn't have anyone he could talk about his friends to. Maurice and Hayden were always there for him, he maintained, but sometimes it was important for him to vent about them, rather than to them. He'd been unable to do that lately. Until now. He told Tara about Hayden's assault of the man on the train.

'He's seemed a bit off since then' said Jet Tea. 'I reckon he's worried about getting done for it, but I doubt anything will happen. It would have happened by now.'

'Hayden always seemed a bit closed off to me' said Tara, 'like he was keeping something important locked up. It doesn't really surprise me, if I'm honest.'

'We've all got our theories' laughed Jet Tea. He then went on to tell her about Maurice's run-in with the security guard.

'Jesus Christ' said Tara. 'Hasn't he tried to press charges?'

'He says he looked into it' said Jet Tea. 'But

there were a couple of witnesses saying he provoked the guy, called him a cunt or something.'

Tara nodded. 'That sounds like Maurice' she laughed.

They drank some more; Jet Tea caught sight of the late hour. He'd had half a bottle of wine and two cans of lager, plus the beer he drank in the pub. This was no good; he was supposed to be driving. His senses were beginning to get a little hazy. He got up to go to the fridge. 'More wine for me' laughed Tara from the sofa. 'You uncultured wanker!'

But things seemed a lot more normal than they had in a while. They were laughing at something. Jet Tea was too drunk to remember exactly what.

It was dark, but he had no trouble seeing her as he moved closer. She looked up at him and whispered something. It felt completely natural yet somehow strange at the same time.

'Oi.'

Jet Tea faded into consciousness. A vague memory hit him; he was staring into the fridge, jovially telling Tara to 'shut up' as she threw a wine cork at him from the sofa. His surroundings slowly introduced themselves.

With difficulty, he turned his head away from the ceiling to the direction of Tara's voice. There she lay; completely naked, the crumpled duvet embroiled around her legs. She was staring at him intently.

''Ello' he said. Then he realised how calm he was feeling. His head was throbbing and his neck ached, for some reason, but he couldn't deny that he hadn't felt this serene in a very, very long time indeed.

'How are you feeling?' asked Tara.

Jet Tea managed a shrug. He beheld Tara's naked body; a sight he never thought he'd ever get to see again. She was perfect from head to toe. Her long hair which, now he thought about it, was the first thing he'd fallen in love with, was a mess, but it only enhanced her perfection. Her body was sleek and youthful, despite her age. Everything about her was enough to engage every physical and emotional arousal in any fully-functioning, heterosexual male. Jet Tea himself had gone through hell desperately chasing after this level of beauty in recent weeks, now here it was - in the last place he thought of looking. And to know her; that only served to enhance her desirability beyond count. She was intelligent, funny, honest, caring and there was nobody like her on the planet. He'd spent hundreds of mornings just like this one, reminding himself of that.

But he didn't love her now.

He didn't even attempt to lie to himself on that matter. He had loved Tara, from the pit of his stomach, but not any more. Furthermore that look on her face reassured him that she held no intention of rekindling anything. That was a profound relief. They'd both changed as people long before they parted ways. Jet Tea could never admit that back then, but he had no difficulty doing so now.

'How about you?' he asked.

Tara mimicked his shrug. 'I don't think we should do that again' she said.

'Good idea' said Jet Tea, with a grin. 'Sorry about that.'

'Not at all' she laughed. 'My pleasure.'

He turned away from her and stared at the ceiling for what seemed like an hour. It was plain white, with vague brushstrokes embedded in the paintwork. He knew it well. It didn't distort or change colour, the starkness of it didn't become animated or drift apart to reveal something dreaded and intangible beyond. Jet Tea didn't feel himself gradually drifting as he stared.

The ceiling remained stark and white. Jet Tea smiled.

An intrusive beep brought him out of his peace. He sat up and glanced over; a partially-filled wine glass stood beside him on the bedside table, an empty beer can next to that. On the carpet sat a crumpled, probably used condom and next to that, his mobile phone. Was it Gemma? Carefully avoiding the condom, he reached for his phone. He'd received twenty-two missed calls and a text message.

The text was from Maurice, not Gemma. It consisted of just two words, and Jet Tea had absolutely no difficulty understanding either of them;

Hayden. Suicide.

The Departure

Tara hadn't been on Jet Tea's mind much at all in the few days since their drunken night together; which more or less put him back in a state of recent normality. He hadn't avoided her, of course. As well as his physical achievement, that evening had been a success in other areas; amidst his fruitless pursuit of absolutely anyone who lacked male genitalia, he'd forgotten more than just Tara herself, he'd also forgotten how good she was for him. Letting off steam about the unfortunate scrapes his friends had gotten into recently had really helped to clear his mind. He felt more focused, more level headed lately. Although an irritating niggle at the back of his mind kept suggesting that Niall's disembodied magical head was on to something, after all. If the supposed curse was more than simply the ravings of a lunatic, then he'd beaten it.

Two days after that night at hers, Jet Tea and Tara had met for coffee. They never even did that when they were together. They had to, this time. He had to talk about Hayden to someone other than Maurice. He didn't call or text her at all after that, but they'd parted amicably. They even mustered a couple of good-natured jokes about their alcohol-induced decision, managing to avoid tiptoeing around the topic.

The real reason he hadn't thought about her much was simple; Hayden. Why did he do it? How come he'd never said anything to them before? They were supposed to be best friends. Just when Jet Tea had finally achieved a long sought-after sense of inner peace, his friend goes and does this; throws all previous perception of good and bad, hope and despair out the window and confirms that, retroactively, they can't have been close friends at all. What sort of friend would keep feelings as strong as those from someone? His inability to work out whether he was angry, upset, sorry or guilty paradoxically made him feel all of those things.

But it didn't matter; today was Hayden's day. It was time to be brave, whatever he was feeling.

Jet Tea didn't sleep well, so that morning he

awoke earlier than usual. He didn't have a job any more, so he walked into town just to kill some time and decided to pop into HMV. He couldn't spend much; he had plans for the relatively large amount of money he'd managed to save, but it wouldn't hurt to browse.

He skipped past the cluster of Pixies albums, as he'd come to understand that it is a terrible idea to stand in a music shop and look at CDs by a certain band when one is wearing said band's t-shirt; passers-by would naturally assume that he was an obsessive fan with no other musical interests. Even though that wasn't quite the case, it has long since been established that Jet Tea does care what others think of him. He knew this more than ever, today.

Jet Tea stalked the shiny, plastic CD aisles, keenly darting his head every which way in the hope that something special among the plethora of dross would reveal itself to him. He picked up an album by someone called Arlo Guthrie; *Alice's Restaurant*. He semi-recognised the name of the artist, but it was the subject matter of the album's title that appealed to him foremost, so he took it with him and continued his search.

Joy Division. He wasn't sure if he had all of their records; surely such a seminal band hadn't only released three? Either way he flicked through the selection, but didn't hold out much hope. He'd read a bit about Joy Division -as much as he could manage- since getting into them, and it didn't seem right to think about their music on this particular day.

A girl sidled up next to him, seemingly only there to look at the CDs in that section. She was pretty; deep, dyed-red hair that was almost auburn in the dim light of the shop hung neck height and splendidly framed her big, attractive eyes and honest-looking smile. She had a natural skip in her step and was slightly shorter than Jet Tea. She turned to him.

'Nice t-shirt' she said in an exotic accent that Jet Tea couldn't place but was most probably European. 'I love Pixies.'

Jet Tea looked up, hesitantly. 'Sorry?'

'I said I love the Pixies' she repeated.

He nodded, politely. He wasn't particularly in the mood for a conversation with a stranger, right now.

'Thanks' he replied. 'Me too, obviously.'

'I recognise you' said the girl. 'You've been in the Treaty a few times, haven't you?'

He noticed the odd tattoo on her neck; that of a rodent-like creature.

'Yeah it's my local' he said.

'It's a nice pub' she replied, smiling. 'I'm going

there later, actually.'

Jet Tea squinted. The Treaty, a nice pub? What on Earth was she talking about?

'I'm sorry' he said with a polite formality. 'I've got a bit of a heavy day today and I just need to be on my own. No offence.'

Her smile waned. 'Oh, okay' she said. 'Not to worry.'

At that she left, and Jet Tea continued browsing, thankful for the solitude.

He met Maurice on the way. It was the first time they'd seen each other since the dreaded text message. It had only been a few days, but the over-hanging sombre mood surrounding them made it feel like the reunion of two acquaintances from long ago who never really liked each other in the first place.

'Should I be wearing this t-shirt?' asked Jet Tea.

Maurice laughed weakly. 'I doubt Hayden would mind' he replied, followed by a short pause. 'I'm sorry about the brevity of my text, by the way' he continued. 'I was just in such a panic. It was a miracle I managed to type anything. Why didn't you answer your phone?'

'It doesn't matter' said Jet Tea.

'Fair enough. Either way, I can see why you misunderstood.'

Hayden smiled up at his friends with tired effort from his bed. He'd been discharged that morning; his left leg was bandaged and his neck marked with scratches and bruises. Maurice sat on the end of the bed, Jet Tea remained standing. He was unable to hide his morose expression; subconsciously, he didn't want Hayden to forget that he wasn't the only person he'd brought pain to. The look behind his mother's impressive smile as she answered the door even attested to that. Maurice was, as ever, the first to speak.

'So what's the verdict with the police?'

Hayden took a deep breath. 'Community service' he croaked. 'I was too stupid and paranoid to even consider that possibility.'

'Is that all?' said Jet Tea.

'Yep. A hundred hours' said Hayden. 'Fifty for the attack, another fifty for running away. I haven't been sentenced yet, but everyone's saying that'll be the outcome. Turns out there was a witness on that train that saw the guy harassing me, hence the lenience.'

Maurice smiled. 'Who?'

'I have no idea' Hayden replied. 'I'm fucking

grateful though.'

'How come they just phoned you?' Maurice continued. 'Why didn't they just go to your house or work and arrest you straight up?'

'Turns out they just wanted to question me at first' said Hayden. 'Not arrest me.'

Jet Tea could stand no more. What Hayden had done -or at least tried to do- was far more important than idle chat about witnesses and community service. Maurice of all people shouldn't be sidestepping that.

'What happened that night?' Jet Tea asked.

With an embarrassed sigh, Hayden told them.

After running away from the police, he found himself at the edge of the park. It was dark in there, while all the surrounding roads were well lit (he'd been mugged in that ample lighting twice in his life; the muggers weren't deterred then, but he knew that if he continued to tread there now the police would spot him in minutes). There was no other option but to head into the park, so he did.

In the brief period of calm that he was allowed, he began to cry. It would only be minutes before he was found. They'd somehow managed to catch him at the pub, so why wouldn't they assume he'd run into darkness? Hayden was no criminal; he did not come prepared with an effective getaway strategy, all he had going for him were his base instincts; run away and hide. He strolled through the twilit park, afraid not simply of justice but also of the darkness itself. There was a reason nobody came in here at night. The autumnally-jagged trees reached out to him threateningly as he wondered what might be lurking behind them. There was a mild wind, so if anything stirred in the blackness he wouldn't know as the sound would be lost beneath the breeze. His pace quickened, almost involuntarily, until before long he came upon a prominent tree in the centre of the grounds. It was taller than most of the others, and it seemed to be the place he was headed after all. The dark, nasty air, filled with impending tragedy, clawed at him. This was a hopeless world; where even nature held a sinister glare at all who passed through it. This darkness would not yield, there was no sunrise.

He began to climb the tree in an almost hypnotic trance. Once he had reached a considerable height, he stopped. He leant on a thick branch and removed his jumper, tying one end to the branch, the other around his neck. Stretched out to its longest possible arm-span, the jumper managed an impressive length. It was either him or them, and it looked like humanity was going nowhere.

Hayden closed his eyes tightly, took a deep breath and jumped.

The branch snapped off instantaneously. It wasn't as strong as it looked. Hayden fell, probably squealed, and landed on the mercifully soft grass. A moment's furious embarrassment followed. That hadn't worked, then. A flash of flickering light roused him to his feet; the police were near. He got up and ran; stopping momentarily to untie the large, dismembered branch dragging behind him.

Against his will, Hayden found himself back on the high street, exposed. His feet ached from running and his neck was killing him. His conviction remained, though. He crossed the road and ran to the building on the other side; a multi-storey car park. Twenty-four hour access; the one building he could get into and reach the top of at this time of night. With the approaching police car hot on his heels, he ducked through the doorway and darted desperately up the spiral staircase until he reached the top.

He found himself standing on a ledge, breathing heavily and looking down. What decisions had he made in his life that had brought him to this point? A smiling child, running to cuddle his mum when she arrived home from work. Waking Dad up at eight in the morning

331

because they were going to the zoo that day. Now he was a grown man, drunk and crying into the night, ready to end his life in an undignified splatter against the dirty concrete. When did that happen?

The police car was below. It had stopped; presumably through the realisation of what their quarry was about to do. Hayden squeezed his eyes closed to try and push his parents out of his mind. Wonder what time mum will start worrying? He'd told her to say he wasn't in if the police came knocking. What about when they knocked this time?

Jet Tea and Maurice arrived in his head. He suddenly felt peaceful. They would be leaving soon. Time to behave in kind. He unscrewed his features and stepped forward.

He began to hum; *Let's Go Fly a Kite* and without thinking he toppled over the edge. It was quiet. Something hard broke his fall instantly. There was an audible crunching sound as it did. A double-decker bus had unwittingly pulled up below him as he fell; he'd landed on it, considerably severing the length of his descent. Was somebody laughing?

Hayden could recall little after that.

'You're a fucking idiot' said Maurice.

'I know that now' Hayden replied, irritably.

'Are you going to try and do that again?'

'Never' he said without hesitation.

'It's like the world was protecting you' said Jet Tea. Hayden frowned.

'Never mind me' he said, his amicable tone hampered under his gruff voice. 'How are you doing? How did it go with that wizard?'

Jet Tea smiled. 'Not bad, I reckon.'

'Where did you run off to?' asked Maurice.

'Tara's.'

A mutual grin filled the room, nothing else needed to be said.

'Do you two fancy a pint?' asked Hayden, of all people.

'I'm sorry?' replied Maurice.

'I haven't been out in days' said Hayden. 'I really need some fresh air.'

Jet Tea glanced fondly up into his own thoughts. 'Does it have to be beer?' he asked. 'Can we go for a coffee?'

Hayden managed a shrug. 'I suppose it's a bit early.'

'On the bright side' said Maurice, nodding at

Hayden's crutches which leant beside his bed, 'if any more posh twats have a go at your bag at least you won't need a golf club.'

'Won't be doing much running away though, will I?' replied Hayden.

They left, after a bit of difficulty getting down the stairs, and made their way to the nearest coffee shop, stopping obediently at the instruction of the glowing, red man standing idly upon his black podium at the road crossing as a purple car drove by. A bunch of flowers lay beside them, tied to the corner of the bollard. A man and his young son had been killed here recently, mown down by a drunk driver. Their memorial a meagre bundle of flowers, trampled on by oblivious passers by and splattered with the mud, grit and engine oil from puddles splashed on them by other drivers. Hayden stared over at it and felt sorry.

The sky was pale grey, almost white. The three of them arrived at the coffee house and sat down. Jet Tea got up to make his order at the counter but a smiley young waitress gestured for him to remain in his seat and took their order at the table instead.

'Did you finish recording?' Hayden asked Maurice.

'Nearly' he replied. 'There's just one bit of vocal giving me grief.'

'Can't wait to hear it. How about you, Jet Tea? Got a new job yet?'

Jet Tea opened his mouth to speak, but a tray of coffee cups appeared in front of him. The waitress placed all of their drinks on the table and left. Jet Tea proceeded.

'No, I'm not getting one. I'm moving to New Zealand.'

Hayden's cup halted on its journey to his mouth. 'I'm sorry?'

Jet Tea shrugged. 'Yeah. I don't know. I just like the sound of New Zealand.'

'Have you been there?' asked Maurice. 'I mean, fair play and all that, I think you need to get away from here, but do you know anything about New Zealand?'

'I know there's a lot of work going for decent chefs' he said.

'Why New Zealand?' asked Hayden.

Jet Tea didn't want to say. 'Why not?'

'It's a bit far. How long are you going for?'

He shrugged again. 'As long as I enjoy it, I guess.'

Three weeks went by. Maurice finished the last of his vocals and had managed to acquire an EP launch party in Kilburn, hosted and funded by a promising, up and coming promotional company. At the party he drank a bottle and a half of red wine, changed the lyrics to all of his songs to make them about his penis and called the head of the company a paedophile. Two days later he received a polite email from them informing him that they wouldn't be distributing his record on this occasion.

Hayden's leg was a lot better; he still needed crutches for the time being, but he could more or less keep up a decent pace on them now. His neck still hurt occasionally, if ever he turned his head too suddenly, but those occasions were few and far between. He'd also received his sentencing, and the assumption of community service had proven to be correct. He wasn't even dreading it, as his best friends were both going to be off soon and Hayden was rather looking forward to having something to fill up his free time; in all the distraction of angry, drunken facebook rants about soldiers, smashing the skulls of middle class men and watching Maurice's trouserless victory dance, he'd quite forgotten to make other friends. He'd have to think of something productive to do until they returned or he saved enough money to join one of them.

They were at the airport now. Jet Tea and Hayden had been there for an hour, making small talk and trying with too much self-consciousness to reminisce on times gone by, because that's how departures are supposed to work. Hayden waxed nostalgically about the time they visited Vienna on their travels through Europe and he'd drunkenly mistook a brothel for his hostel, punching Jet Tea in the mouth when he tried to help him. But that's another story.

Maurice hadn't said anything about being late and Jet Tea was growing concerned that they'd miss each other. He didn't want his last words to his best friend to be 'McDonalds, bitch.'

Thankfully, Maurice darted into view, looking confusedly every which way before eventually spotting his friends. Punching the air in success, he jogged over to them.

'Sorry I'm late.'

'Why do you have your guitar?' asked Hayden.

'I'm going to see if I can buy a ticket to Berlin after Jet Tea goes' he replied.

'Really? Nice' Jet Tea replied.

Hayden nodded solemnly. 'Where's the rest of your stuff?' he asked.

'Here' said Maurice, defiantly revealing a small rucksack dangling over his shoulder.

'What have you got in there?' asked Jet Tea.

'Three t-shirts and a banana. I'll acquire any other necessary items once I'm there.'

'I dare say that's all you'll need' said Hayden, laughing.

A musical chime echoed around the room, and a beautiful, smoky female voice followed it, urging passengers to begin boarding. It's almost as though she's enticing people to other corners of the globe, thought Maurice. Like a siren. Why else would they precede her words with music?

They stood up. Hayden huffed. 'I suppose I'm getting the bus back by myself then' he groaned jovially. 'You cunts.'

'You're the cunt' said Maurice. 'That's why you're on crutches in the first place.'

They laughed. 'And Jet Tea's a cunt for fucking off to a country he's never been to and probably can't even spell.'

'I can't spell England either' said Jet Tea. 'So get a room, comedian.'

Maurice and Hayden smiled at each other confusedly. 'You're still a cunt' said Maurice.

'Whatever' Jet Tea replied. 'Some people are born cunts, some people become cunts' he said, whimsically. 'But if you really know you're a cunt then you're gonna be a cunt all your life.'

He giggled at his friends and raised a single hand to bid them farewell, before turning away and dragging his suitcase through the gate. Maurice caught sight of Hayden's dampening eyes in his periphery and placed a hand softly on his back.

'I know, mate' he said comfortingly. 'I know.'

Jet Tea sat by the window, hoping that the seat next to him would remain empty and prepping himself to lower his standards when his first in-flight meal arrived. He'd never been on so long a plane journey before, so curiosity was preventing him from dreading it too much. Before long the plane began to move.

He closed his eyes in discomfort as the plane hit the runway; he hated that bit. But it didn't last long and soon enough they were airborne. He looked out of the window, trying to see behind him. England fell away beneath the clouds and was gone forever.

A shudder irritated him out of his thoughts.

Turbulence. Another one, worse than the first. Then the shudders kept coming. The plane rocked in all directions but Jet Tea was too gobsmacked to make a commotion. This was bad. Why was nobody else responding? What was going on? He tried to look around; nope. Nobody else was panicking, or even shuffling in their seats. Why hadn't the pilot made an announcement of some kind? In the corner of his eye he noticed the sky begin to change colour.

Was the plane crashing? Exploding? Still no one else seemed remotely bothered as the walls and seats began to part and spread, completely letting in the brilliant array of colour. Jet Tea could feel the incredible speed of the plane and, almost overwhelmed, he nonetheless managed to hold his hands up in front of his face. They seemed to be emitting flakes; particles of skin were literally drifting away from his fingers, disappearing into the glare. They were parting too, all of him was. He saw himself gracefully coming to pieces as the plane rumbled and colour began to flood and shroud everything else in sight. He must be experiencing real magic, he thought. Actually, it was much more than that. He began to feel more and more euphoric as a warm sense of worth overcame him. Chasing a smile to the furthest corner of the planet tends to do that. His form ceased to be; he was becoming magic. Magic itself. Gemma would definitely be impressed by that...

Joe Gardner grew up in Hayes, West London. He studied English Literature at the University of Reading and currently lives in Soho. *The Life and Loves of Jet Tea* is his first novel.

Joe's lifelong ambition is to write an author's note more interesting than this one.

All characters appearing in this work are fictitious. Any resemblance to real persons, living or dead, is purely coincidental.